FLAMES OF DISASTER!

Facing into the wind, Nancy looked south. First she saw smoke rising from the ground. Then she saw flames spreading across the horizon.

Joe clenched and unclenched his fists. "They set this fire on purpose—and it's heading this way!"

"To get rid of us," Nellie added.

"But that's crazy!" Mick exclaimed. "That fire will kill every living thing in its path! It could ruin hundreds of acres of outback."

Nancy kept her eyes on the fire. Flames kept racing toward them at an amazing speed. The sky was already filled with smoke—the flames crackled more and more loudly every second.

"You guys, the wind is building. It's blowing the fire out of control!" Nancy cried. "In a few minutes those flames are going to be right on top of us!"

Nancy Drew & Hardy Boys SuperMysteries

DOUBLE CROSSING
A CRIME FOR CHRISTMAS
SHOCK WAVES
DANGEROUS GAMES
THE LAST RESORT
THE PARIS CONNECTION
BURIED IN TIME
MYSTERY TRAIN
BEST OF ENEMIES
HIGH SURVIVAL
NEW YEAR'S EVIL
TOUR OF DANGER
SPIES AND LIES
TROPIC OF FEAR
COURTING DISASTER
HITS AND MISSES
EVIL IN AMSTERDAM
DESPERATE MEASURES
PASSPORT TO DANGER
HOLLYWOOD HORROR
COPPER CANYON CONSPIRACY
DANGER DOWN UNDER

Available from ARCHWAY Paperbacks

A
Nancy Drew
AND
Hardy Boys
SUPER MYSTERY™

DANGER DOWN UNDER

Carolyn Keene

AN ARCHWAY PAPERBACK
Published by POCKET BOOKS

New York   London   Toronto   Sydney   Tokyo   Singapore

This book is a work of fiction. Names, characters, places and incidents are products of the author's imagination or are used fictitiously. Any resemblance to actual events or locales or persons, living or dead, is entirely coincidental.

AN ARCHWAY PAPERBACK *Original*

An Archway Paperback published by
POCKET BOOKS, a division of Simon & Schuster Inc.
1230 Avenue of the Americas, New York, NY 10020

Copyright © 1995 by Simon & Schuster Inc.
Produced by Mega-Books, Inc.

ISBN: 0-671-88460-3

First Archway Paperback printing March 1995

10 9 8 7 6 5 4 3 2 1

NANCY DREW, THE HARDY BOYS, AN ARCHWAY PAPERBACK and colophon are registered trademarks of Simon & Schuster Inc.

A NANCY DREW AND HARDY BOYS SUPERMYSTERY is a trademark of Simon & Schuster Inc.

Cover art by Brian Kotzky

Printed in the U.S.A.

IL 6+

DANGER DOWN UNDER

Chapter

One

N ANCY, I DON'T THINK we'll *ever* get through customs," George Fayne said, stretching tiredly. She scanned the lines of tourists waiting to have their passports stamped. "At the rate we're moving, it'll be time to leave Australia and fly back to the States, and we won't have seen anything but the Sydney airport."

Nancy Drew stifled a yawn, then pushed her backpack ahead as the line inched forward. "I know what you mean. We've been waiting over an hour, and that's after sitting through two movies and three meals on the plane. I don't even know what day it is anymore."

"I know today's Friday, but what's the season?" George asked. "It was cold when we left River Heights, but here in March it's late summer." She ran her fingers through her short, dark curls. "Oh, well. I'm sure Mick will help us get oriented."

Just the mention of Mick Devlin's name caused Nancy to blush. "I, uh, hope so." She opened her shoulder bag and rummaged around inside. "Where's that customs form the flight attendant gave us to fill out?"

"In your hand," George pointed out dryly. "You must be nervous about seeing Mick again, huh?"

Nancy smiled. She should have known that George would see through her in a second. "I guess I am," she admitted. "It's just that . . ." She hesitated, searching for the right words.

From the first second they'd met, there had been something special between Nancy and the gorgeous Aussie. She had met him when she was traveling in Europe with George and George's cousin, Bess Marvin. When they'd returned to the U.S., Nancy thought she'd never see Mick again. She'd been totally surprised when he showed up at a friend's wedding in Japan. Mick hadn't made a secret of the fact that he was still crazy about her, but . . .

"Mick and I settled things when we were in Tokyo. We're friends, that's all," Nancy said firmly. "He's an amazing guy, but nothing is more important to me than Ned and the things I love in River Heights." Ned Nickerson was Nancy's longtime boyfriend.

George raised an eyebrow at her, but all she said was, "Okay. I'm curious about what's so important that we needed to fly all this way to help out."

"You know as much as I do," Nancy said with a shrug. "A friend of his needs our help in the outback."

"Sounds like my kind of trip," George said. Nancy knew that George loved hiking and roughing it. The rugged and largely unpopulated Australian outback, like the American West, would be perfect. "Hey! Didn't you say Frank and Joe sent you a postcard from Australia?" George asked.

"Yes," Nancy said, "but they didn't say where they were traveling." She smiled, thinking about the Hardy brothers. They were the only people Nancy knew who loved to solve mysteries as much as she did.

She blinked and realized she and George were at the customs desk. "At last! It's our turn. Come on."

Emerging on the other side of customs, Nancy began to feel jittery about Mick again and quickly brushed a hand through her shoulder-length reddish blond hair. "I hope Mick is here," she said, scanning the crowd. "He said he'd—"

"Nancy! George!"

The sound of Mick's deep voice made Nancy stop short. She spotted him pushing through the crowd. He was grinning at her, and Nancy couldn't help grinning back. One look at his amazing green eyes, and she felt a warm tingle spread through her from head to toe.

"Mick!" Nancy dropped her backpack as Mick caught her up in a huge hug. When he finally let her go, she felt breathless.

"It's great to see you," Mick said in a husky voice.

"Same here," she told him, feeling slightly giddy. He was tanned, and his blond hair was bleached from the sun. In his jeans and white T-shirt, he looked more gorgeous than ever as he gave George a hug.

"Where's your friend, the one who needs our help?" George asked, glancing around.

"Nellie Mabo," Mick supplied. "She goes to university with me, but right now she's with her tribe in the Queensland outback."

"Tribe?" Nancy raised an eyebrow at Mick. "Is Nellie an Aborigine?"

Mick nodded. "Her people have been in Australia for forty thousand years, give or take a few thousand."

"So what is it that she needs help with?" George asked.

"We're flying to meet her in the outback in a little while," Mick said. He picked up the girls' backpacks and slung one over each shoulder. "Come on. I'll explain everything over lunch."

"I wish we could spend more time in Sydney," George commented an hour later. She, Nancy, and Mick were seated in a restaurant called the Rocks Café. The waitress had just placed a meat pie, a platter of barbecued beef, and some grilled vegetables in front of them.

"I'll say," Nancy agreed. "Modern and old-fashioned at the same time." She gazed out the window at the narrow, cobbled street lined with pubs, cafés, and shops. Behind the stone and brick buildings, tall skyscrapers curved around Sydney's harbor and filled the downtown area.

Mick grinned at Nancy. "I always thought you'd love it here. Was I right?"

Nancy looked down at her meat pie, feeling her cheeks turn red. "Tell us about Nellie Mabo," she said, abruptly changing the subject.

Mick's expression immediately became serious. "Nellie and I have been good friends ever since we did a project together for a class last year." He took a bite of barbecued beef, then said, "I've learned a lot about the Aborigines from her."

"So what kind of trouble is she in?" George asked, taking a sip of soda.

"Actually, her whole tribe is in trouble." Mick took a deep breath before continuing. "I guess I should start at the beginning. Nellie's grandfather is a leader of the Yungi—that's their tribe. He raised Nellie after her parents died, when she was little. Anyway, one of the things he's responsible for is keeping the tribe's tjuringa."

"What's that?" Nancy asked.

"The traditional Aborigine way of life is closely linked to nature. They believe that the earth was in a sleeping state until the Ancestors sang it to life," Mick began.

"Sang it to life?" George repeated. "I'm not sure I understand."

"The Ancestors were spiritual beings who traveled the country, scattering words and musical notes along with their footprints. As they traveled, the land and animals and people sprang to life. Kind of like a musical Genesis."

"That's really interesting," George said, her brown eyes gleaming.

Mick nodded. "That whole process is called the Dreaming. Each Ancestor's path mapped out the land of his tribe, and every tribe has a different Dreaming. Nellie told me that the Yungis belong to the Honey Ant Dreaming. That means their ancestral father somehow contained the spirit of the honey ant."

"But what does this have to do with the tjuringa?" Nancy wondered aloud.

"Each tribe keeps a board carved with songs and patterns that show the wanderings of its Dreamtime Ancestor," Mick explained.

"And that's the tjuringa?" George guessed.

Mick nodded. "It's sacred. Only people who are initiated into the tribe are allowed to see it. Nellie told me her grandfather keeps it carefully stored away." He frowned and stabbed at his barbecued beef with his fork. "But that didn't stop someone from stealing it."

"Oh, no!" Nancy said, staring at Mick.

"That's what I said when Nellie told me about it," Mick said grimly. "A week ago the tjuringa disappeared. Nellie and her grandfather haven't been able to find it anywhere, and they didn't want to go to the police."

"Why not?" George asked.

"A lot of Aborigines feel they've gotten a raw deal from the government in the past."

"Kind of the way some Native Americans feel back home," George said.

"Yeah," Mick agreed. "Anyway, Nellie's grandfather doesn't want to have anything to do with the authorities."

George looked up from her meat pie. "But he doesn't mind getting help from two girls who live half a continent away and know almost nothing about the Aborigines' way of life?"

"Actually, Nellie almost wasn't able to convince her grandfather to let you come," Mick said. "But I've visited the Yungi community a lot since Nellie and I became friends, and her grandfather trusts me now. When I told him that I knew someone who could solve mysteries that baffled the police, he agreed to let you search for the tjuringa."

Nancy felt flattered and hoped she wouldn't let him and Nellie down.

"Nancy, look!" George shouted above the droning engine of the four-seater propeller plane and pointed out the window. She was sitting next to the pilot, while Nancy and Mick were perched on seats just behind. The rest of the tiny plane was packed with supplies being flown to the outback.

Nancy gazed in the direction George indicated and spotted a group of kangaroos bounding among the eucalyptus trees and grasslands below. "Amazing! I haven't stopped looking since we took off from the Sydney airport," she said, grinning.

Mick and the pilot, a lanky man in his thirties named Roger Lang, had been pointing out the sights as they flew. They'd gone north along the coast before turning inland, where the more populated areas gave way to a strip of thickly forested mountains. Then the lush green hills flattened out to the immense, dry outback that stretched endlessly in all directions. For the last hour Nancy had caught sight of only one or two small towns.

"I don't think I've ever seen so much wide-open space," Nancy commented. "The outback seems to go on forever. It's spectacular."

"Most Australians live along the coasts. Huge parts of the interior are only sparsely settled, so flying is the best way to get around," Mick explained.

While he spoke, Nancy kept her eyes on the wild, dry land below. "What's that?" she asked, pointing to a spot in the distance where she saw a tinge of green rising out of the scrub and dust.

"Comet Creek National Park," Roger told them. "Got some bonzer gorges thereabouts. You ought to be goin' walkabout down there, eh?"

Nancy was still getting used to Roger's way of talking, but she knew that *bonzer* meant "great" and *walkabout* was what Australians called taking a walk away from it all.

"Comet Creek runs through a series of gorges," Mick explained. "It's a real oasis. The Yungi community is right outside the national park, near the town of Flat Hill. That's where we'll be staying."

As Roger flew closer, Nancy got a better look at the lush gorges. Near one was a small rise in the land, with a town that seemed to spring right out of the top of it. Buildings stretched for a few blocks wide and several blocks long. An occasional house or station, an Australian ranch, dotted the land outside the town and park.

"Nellie told me that the town's permanent population is only about five hundred people. Mostly suppliers for the sheep stations farther out and people who cater to tourists going into the national park," Mick explained. "Plus a few hundred Aborigines in the Yungi settlement."

In a matter of minutes the plane touched down on a small airstrip about a half mile east of the town. "Wow. The air smells great," George said, lugging her backpack from the plane while Mick and Roger began unloading the boxes of supplies.

"Mmm." Nancy dropped her own pack and took in the clean, earthy scents. She turned as a battered green truck drove up to the airstrip, stirring up a cloud of dust. Behind the wheel was a dark-skinned girl who wore a scarf tied around her black curls.

"Nellie!" Mick cried. The truck stopped, and the girl got out. Mick jogged over to her.

"Eh, Mick," Nellie greeted him. She was shorter than Nancy and wore jeans and a work shirt. Nancy was struck by the unhurried way she moved. There was an intelligent glint in her dark eyes as she and

Mick moved over to Nancy and George. Up close, Nancy saw that the scarf in Nellie's hair was bright red, with tie-dyed yellow circles.

"Nancy, George, this is Nellie Mabo," Mick said.

"Afternoon," Nellie greeted them, with a nod.

"Nice to meet you," George said, smiling.

"I hope we can help you and your grandfather," Nancy added.

A slow smile spread across Nellie's wide, round face. "I do, too. Shall we go round to see him?"

After stowing their packs in the back of the truck, Nancy, Mick, and George squeezed into the front seat next to Nellie. Instead of driving up the rise and into Flat Hill, Nellie took a road that led northeast of the town.

"The Yungi community is this way, near the entrance to Comet Creek National Park," Mick said.

"I've got a caravan, what you call a trailer, there, where you two can sleep," Nellie told Nancy and George. "I'll be staying with my granddad."

"And I've got a tent," Mick added.

A few minutes later Nancy spotted rows of houses nestled against some low ridges. Nellie turned onto a side road and stopped the truck in front of a low wooden house in the shade of a eucalyptus tree.

"Granddad?" Nellie called, pushing open the front door. Nancy, Mick, and George followed her inside.

The room they entered was sparsely furnished

with a wooden table and chairs. A few wooden carvings hung on the walls. Sitting at the table was an elderly man in cotton slacks and a plaid shirt with the sleeves cut off. He had curly gray hair, a coarse mustache and beard, and the same wide features and soft eyes as Nellie. For a long moment he didn't say anything. Then finally he gestured for them to sit. "Mick says you'll be able to help us," he said, smiling.

"I hope so," Nancy told him. She decided she might as well get right down to business. "He's told us about the missing tjuringa. Do you have any idea who could have taken it?"

The elderly man gave a slow shake of his head. "I know it could not have been anyone from our tribe. They would not violate a sacred board."

Nancy knew from experience that it was possible for anyone in *any* community to do a terrible thing. But she decided not to say anything yet.

"How about someone from outside your tribe?" George asked.

Nellie turned to Mick and asked, "Have you told them about our conflict with—"

She broke off as a loud knock sounded at the door. Nellie opened the door, and Nancy saw a woman in a cream-colored suit and low-heeled pumps standing there. Despite her tanned, freckled skin and sun-bleached blond hair, the woman looked out of place in the rough outback. Anything but happy, she stormed into the house.

"You're trying to ruin me!" she said, stabbing a finger in Nellie's direction.

"Afternoon, Marian," Nellie said calmly. "Come in, won't you?" Her composed attitude only seemed to make the woman angrier.

"Don't try that friendly act on me," Marian sputtered, taking a threatening step toward Nellie. Her face was almost purple with fury, and her eyes were icy.

"You and your people had better back off," Marian went on. "If you don't, you'll be sorry!"

Chapter

Two

Nancy's whole body tensed as the woman took another step toward Nellie. Mick and George seemed ready to jump into action, too. Mr. Mabo sat so still, Nancy couldn't tell what he was thinking.

"We'll talk about this later, eh?" Nellie said to Marian, still not losing her calm. "I've got more important things on my mind at the moment."

"Oh, yes. That silly tjuringa board of yours," Marian said, rolling her eyes. "Imagine, an entire community in an uproar over a piece of wood."

The woman obviously had no respect for the Yungis' way of life. "Why don't you just get out of here," George muttered.

Marian blinked at her, Nancy, and Mick, as if only just realizing they were there. "Fine," she said, turning back to Nellie. "But you should know that Royce Mining is going to fight you every step of the way on this. And we're going to win!"

With that, the woman left. Through the open door, Nancy saw her kick angrily at a clump of grass her heel had gotten caught in. After climbing into her Range Rover, she banged the door closed and zoomed off.

"Who was that?" George asked.

Nellie closed the door and sat back down at the table. "That was Marian Royce," she answered. "She and her husband, Ian, moved here about six months ago, when they bought an opal mine about three hours' drive south of here. It's very barren there, so Ian and Marian have their office in town."

"She doesn't exactly look like the outdoors type," George commented.

Mick laughed. "From what Nellie's told me, that's the understatement of the year. Apparently Marian hates the outback. That's probably why she and her husband live here in Flat Hill. It sure isn't a big city, but it's something."

Nancy couldn't help wondering why Marian would live in a place she hated, but she had another, more important question on her mind. "What was she talking about when she said she'd fight you every step of the way?" she asked Nellie.

"The Royces violate sacred Yungi land with their mine," Nellie's grandfather answered.

Mick explained, "The Yungi believe that the land should never be disturbed, but there are some sites that are especially sacred. The Royces dug a huge pit right in the middle of a strip of land that's very important."

"Path of the Rainbow Snake," Nellie's grandfather put in.

"No one can undo the damage the mine has brought to our sacred sites, but that is not the only issue," Nellie added. "It is not right for the Royces to profit from our people's land."

"Nellie has been organizing the Yungi community against the Royces," Mick told Nancy and George. "Ian and Marian wouldn't even talk to them about their concerns, so a few weeks ago the Yungis hired a big-time lawyer. Now they're petitioning the Australian government to have the land turned over to them. Aborigines in other parts of Australia have succeeded in getting mining land returned. I guess Marian threw a fit when she found out that might happen to her mine, too."

"Our lawyer is supposed to come here in a few days to meet with the Royces," Nellie said with a sigh. "I may put it off, though. Granddad and I don't have time for Royce Mining now. We've got to put all our effort into finding the tjuringa."

Nancy blinked at Nellie as an idea occurred to her. "Maybe that's what the Royces are counting on," she said. "Marian seemed almost pleased about the chaos the missing tjuringa has been causing."

"So maybe *she* took the board, just to get Nellie off their backs," George said.

"If that's their plan, then the Royces don't know Nellie very well," Mick said, shooting Nellie a broad smile.

Nellie nodded soberly. "Whoever stole our tjuringa does not respect the traditional Yungi way of life," she said. "It could be Ian and Marian Royce."

"I'll check them out as soon as I can," Nancy promised, her attention caught by a wooden carving on the wall. A series of simple lines, circles, and dots, the carving was striking. "That's beautiful," she commented, nodding toward it.

"Nellie made that," Mick said. "It's a bark carving. The shapes are symbols for places, people, and land forms."

"It's a traditional aboriginal art form," Nellie explained. "Those wavy lines are the Comet Creek gorges, and the circles are Aboriginal campsites."

"We Yungi have many ways of expressing ourselves," Nellie's grandfather added. "Mick, you must bring your friends to the corroboree Wednesday night."

"The what?" George asked.

"It's a traditional song and dance fest," Mick explained. "Watching one is an amazing experience."

"Thanks for inviting us," Nancy told Nellie's grandfather. "We'd love to come." Even if they found the tjuringa before then, the corroboree sounded like something she and George shouldn't miss. Her main concern now, though, was how they were going to find a sacred plaque that Nellie's whole tribe hadn't been able to locate.

"Here we are," Mick announced a half hour later. He pulled Nellie's truck to a stop about halfway down Flat Hill's main street. "Nellie told me that Flat Hill was settled in the late 1800s as a supply center for sheep stations around here," Mick went on. "A lot of the old buildings are still standing."

They had passed modern brick and wooden buildings at the edge of town, but here in the center, most of the structures were in the Victorian style.

Mick headed for a three-story building that had round turrets and fancy wooden porches on the second and third floors. "This is the Flat Hill Lodge. They've got the only restaurant in town, so I hope you like it."

"As long as they have food—any food—I'm sure I'll love it," George said.

"The food is pretty good," Mick said. "They get a fair number of hikers and campers on their way to and from the national park, so Regina Bourke, the owner, does her best to keep the customers happy."

"I wouldn't mind calling home," Nancy said. "I promised Dad and Hannah I'd give them a number where they can reach me."

"You can leave the lodge's number," Mick assured her. "Regina's used to receiving messages for people in the area."

"Tell your dad to give my parents the number, too," George said to Nancy.

Mick led the way through the lodge's entrance and into a reception area dominated by a check-in desk and a carved wooden stairway that twisted up to the second floor. Some dusty-looking stuffed birds were arranged on a long, high shelf on one wall. While Nancy used the pay phone next to the check-in desk to call her father, she noticed two people standing near the shelf—a tall man with a sunburned face and a robust woman in an apron. They seemed to be talking about the birds, but Nancy was too busy talking to her father to pay much attention.

"Thanks for waiting, guys," she told Mick and George after she'd hung up. "Let's eat."

Mick led her and George through a doorway to the right of the entrance. The restaurant was casual and Nancy liked it right away. A man wearing a white apron sat reading a paper at a counter that ran along one wall. Wooden booths lined the opposite wall, and a half-dozen round tables filled the space between.

As they seated themselves in a booth, the robust woman Nancy had seen in the lobby came through the doorway. "G'day, Mick," she greeted him cheerily, tucking a strand of her dark hair behind her ear. "Didn't even see you come in. You've brought some friends around this visit, I see."

"Evening, Regina," Mick said with an easy smile. "You were busy talking, so we didn't interrupt. This is Nancy Drew and George Fayne. They're visiting from the U.S."

"Pleased to meet you two. I'm Regina Bourke." The two girls shook hands with the woman, then ordered steaks and french fries. When she'd taken their order, Regina gestured to the man Nancy had noticed at the counter. "Paul, we'll take three steaks and chips over here when you get a chance."

The man nodded. As he turned to get down from his stool, Nancy saw that he was short and thin, with leathery skin, a stubble of graying beard, and the palest blue eyes she had ever seen. All at once he scowled at a man who had just entered the restaurant.

"No-good thief," Paul grumbled. "Thanks to your tricks, you're getting rich off my mine."

The man who'd just entered was in his thirties and seemed quiet and shy. He had short, light brown hair and ruddy cheeks, and wore slacks and a short-sleeved, button-down shirt. "There were no tricks, Paul," the man said, acting uncomfortable. "How many times do Marian and I have to tell you?"

"Pack of lies. Those opals are rightfully mine, and you know it!" Paul spat out. He stormed into the kitchen, and seconds later Nancy heard pots being banged on the stove.

"That must be Ian Royce," she whispered to George and Mick as the man sat at a table on the opposite side of the restaurant from the kitchen.

"Right you are," Regina said, collecting their menus. Lowering her voice, she added, "You'll have to excuse Paul. He used to own the land where

Royce Mining is. Worked that patch of dust for over forty-five years without hitting pay dirt. Finally he sells it, and bingo"—she snapped her fingers to emphasize her point—"Ian and Marian find a vein of black opals first thing."

"Wow. I don't blame Paul for being jealous," George said, glancing toward the kitchen.

Regina nodded. "I don't know if he'll ever get over it." Tucking the menus under her arm, she started toward Ian Royce's table. "G'day, Ian."

His response was muffled by the noise of more people entering the restaurant. When Nancy turned to see them, she practically fell out of the booth. "I don't believe it! Frank and Joe Hardy!"

George whipped around, and her mouth fell open. "What are *you* doing here?"

"Nancy? George?" Frank stared as if he couldn't believe his eyes.

"Amazing!" Joe jogged over to their booth and leaned over to give both girls hugs. "I mean, we've run into you in some pretty faraway places, but this beats them all."

"It must be fate," Nancy said, grinning.

Frank turned to an older man who had come in with them. He was wearing khaki shorts, a short-sleeved shirt, and hiking boots. Despite the tufts of gray in his thick, dark hair, he had a slim, muscular build that made him seem younger. "This is Gil Strickland, a friend of our dad. He's been living in Australia for over twenty years."

"Fell in love with an Aussie woman," Gil said, smiling. "When that didn't work out, I realized

I was in love with the outback. Been here ever since."

"Nice to meet you," Nancy said. "You guys, this is Mick Devlin, a friend of ours." She could feel herself blushing as Mick shook hands with the Hardys. After all, there had always been a special spark between her and Frank, and it made her a little nervous to have Frank meet Mick.

While Frank and Joe squeezed in next to George, Nancy filled them in on the details of the missing tjuringa. "I hope you find it," Gil said, pulling up a chair from another table.

"What about you two?" Mick asked Frank and Joe. "What brings you to Flat Hill?"

Just then Regina Bourke arrived with three platters of steaks and chips, or french fries. "I'll take one of those, too," Joe said. While Frank and Gil gave their orders, Joe answered Mick's question. "Gil runs a company called Outback Adventures. The office is right across the street, actually. He guides people on hikes and camping trips into the outback, including Comet Creek National Park. As long as Frank and I were in Australia, we figured we'd check it out. We just got here this morning."

"Sounds great," George said enthusiastically.

"It used to be—before our trouble started," Gil said, frowning.

"Trouble?" Nancy questioned.

Frank glanced around the restaurant. "Poaching," he said in a low voice. "The gorges of the national park are full of rare animals. Some species can't be found anywhere else in the world."

21

"One of the main reasons people go to Comet Creek is to see the wildlife," Mick said.

"Well, now someone is trying to *kill* the wildlife," Joe said grimly.

"That's disgusting!" George exclaimed. "When did it start?"

"A few days ago I was on an overnight camping trip in the Comet Creek gorges with a group of tourists," Gil said. "We heard shots not far from our camp, and when I went for a look-see, I found a rufous bettong. That's a small creature related to the kangaroo. They're rare outside the gorges." He frowned. "It had been killed."

"Unbelievable," Mick said.

"Firearms are strictly forbidden in the national parks," Gil went on. "I found a few rifle shells nearby, but unfortunately the poacher got away before I could get a look at him."

"What's really strange is that the poacher had started to dig a hole to bury the animal," Frank said. "Gil found some plastic sheeting next to it. He thinks he surprised the person before he was able to wrap the bettong and bury it."

"That's weird," Nancy said, putting down her fork. "The plastic sheeting, I mean. Why would he want to bury the animal?"

Gil explained. "Sounds as if the poacher wanted to make sure none of the other animals could get to the carcass. There's a big black market for dead rare animals, and Australia has thousands of species that aren't found anywhere else in the world.

People will pay top dollar for a rare wallaby or bird that they can stuff. The poacher would come back later and dig the animal up and take the time he needed to skin it."

"I guess those people don't care about leaving enough *live* animals around for other people to appreciate," George said angrily.

"Which is why Gil wants to catch the culprit before he kills anything else," Joe put in. "The main reason we stopped by here is to ask the owner of the lodge if she knows about any collectors who've been around."

Nancy remembered the man Regina Bourke had been talking to in the lobby. "I saw the stuffed birds Regina has. She was just talking to someone about them when we got here."

"Talking 'bout me and my grandfather's dead, stuffed creatures, are you?" Regina Bourke spoke up as she appeared with sodas and plates of food for the Hardys and Gil.

"You guessed it," Gil said good-naturedly. He told Regina about the rufous bettong that had been killed.

"Bad news, that is," she said grimly as she served the food. "All I can say is if there's poaching going on, I bet Dennis Moore's got a hand in it. He's the bloke I was talking to. He's one of the biggest collectors in the country—has connections around the world. Comes up from Melbourne on business and always asks if I'll sell my grandfather's collection to him. Those poor birds were killed long before they became protected species. Can't say I'm crazy about the things, but they were my grandfather's—I'm not about to sell."

"Dennis Moore, eh? Is he staying here at the hotel?" Frank asked.

"He is," Regina answered, putting her tray under her arm. "Give a yell if you need anything else."

As the lodge owner went back into the kitchen, Joe said, "One of the biggest dealers in stuffed animals just happens to be around when a rare bettong is killed. Coincidence?"

"I don't think so," Frank answered. "We'd better see what we can find out about the guy."

"Do the police have any ideas about who else might be responsible?" George asked.

"Not yet," Gil answered. "I handed the shells and plastic sheeting I found near the bettong over to the security people at Comet Creek National Park, but they haven't caught the poacher. All we know so far is that the bullets weren't fired from any standard rifle. Whoever's poaching has a custom-made weapon."

Frank picked up a chip and popped it into his mouth. "Joe and I decided to do some investigating, so it looks as if our vacation is turning into a case. Tomorrow we're leaving for a two-day hike to try to ferret out the poacher. The woman who works for Gil will be going as our guide."

"Daphne Whooten," Gil supplied. "She's out with a client now. And while you three are gone, I'll see what I can find out about Mr. Dennis Moore."

"I wish George and I could help," Nancy said, "but—"

She broke off as a high-pitched, terrified scream rang out from outside. The sound chilled Nancy to the bone, but what she heard next made her feel even worse.

"Oh, no!" someone yelled. "It's dead!"

Chapter
Three

J OE JUMPED UP from his chair. "Frank, come on!"

The brothers pounded toward the inn's entrance, with Gil, Nancy, George, and Mick following. Joe yanked open the front door and raced out to the street. He almost ran into a guy with glasses and a girl who were standing next to a red pickup truck parked in front of the inn. Both had horrified expressions on their faces.

"Ugh!" At first all Joe saw was the blood and flesh. He closed his eyes for a second and gulped back a wave of nausea. When he looked again, he realized that he was staring at the bloodied carcass of a kangaroo that was lying in the open truckbed.

"What kind of idiot would kill a kangaroo?" George burst out.

"Idiot?" a deep voice rang out. "You can keep your insults to yourself, thank you."

Joe had been so stunned by the sight of the dead animal that he hadn't realized a third person was there. Now he saw that a young guy with sandy hair and a beard was next to the driver's door, staring at George with disdain. He wore work clothes and boots and stood with one elbow propped on the truck's open window.

"Daphne, what's going on here?" Gil demanded, striding over to the girl. "Who screamed?"

The girl didn't answer Gil. She was staring at the bearded man, her gray eyes flashing with anger. "Did you have to bring that here, Tracker?"

Joe couldn't stop staring at the girl. Even in hiking boots, cut-off shorts, and a T-shirt, she was gorgeous. She was almost as tall as he was, with a slender build and chin-length reddish brown hair that caught the sun. There was a spirited glimmer in her blue eyes that Joe couldn't help admiring.

Daphne, eh? For the first time, Joe noticed the kangaroo that was stitched to the flap of her red backpack—the logo for Outback Adventures. *She* was Gil's employee? This investigation was going to be more fun than he'd expected.

"You know as well as I do that these wallabies are a nuisance," Tracker shot back. He crossed his arms over his chest and swaggered toward Daphne. "This one wrecked one of my fences. It took me half the day to round up my sheep. Now that I'm rid of the pest, I thought maybe Regina would want it for tonight's evening special."

"You mean, *eat* it?" The man with glasses spoke up for the first time. He was about twenty-five, with short blond hair, pale eyebrows, and round cheeks that were completely drained of color.

Tracker opened his mouth to say something else, but before he could, Gil stepped in between him and Daphne. "Will someone tell me what's going on!"

Daphne turned to Gil and said, "Harold and I were going to stop in for a soda after our bush walk. As we arrived, Tracker drove up with"—she nodded toward the dead kangaroo—"this."

"I'm the one who screamed," Harold added, pushing his glasses up on his nose. "I'm afraid I'm not used to this sort of thing."

Tracker snorted, and Gil turned to him angrily. "Everyone around here knows you've been fined for killing excessive numbers of wallabies. Keep it up, and you'll be in real trouble!"

Joe knew that kangaroos were considered pests in some parts of Australia, but apparently Tracker had gone overboard in dealing with the problem. Joe caught his brother's reaction to the mention of fines. Frank didn't say anything, but he was taking in every inch of Tracker and his truck. When Joe noticed Frank staring at something inside the cab, Joe checked, too. He immediately spotted the gun rack behind the driver's seat. Three rifles were in it.

Joe angled closer, trying to see if any of them were custom made, but Tracker strode past him and got into his truck. He said to Gil, "This is a free country, mate. You can't tell me what to do." A second later the truck peeled off down the street and around a corner.

"He seemed in an awful hurry to get out of here," Frank commented. "He didn't even wait to try to sell the wallaby to the restaurant."

"If that's what he was doing," Joe put in. "Maybe what he really intended to do was sell the wallaby to Dennis Moore. Did you get the feeling he didn't want us to see those rifles?"

Daphne gave Joe and Frank a blank look, then turned to Gil. "You think Tracker shot the bettong?"

"We'll do our best to find out," Joe told her, stepping forward with a smile. "I'm Joe Hardy, and this is my brother, Frank."

"Frank, Joe, this is Daphne Whooten, the guide who works with me," Gil said. "They've offered to help catch the poacher, Daphne. I thought you could lead them on a two-day hike into the gorges to check."

Daphne nodded and scrutinized Frank and Joe. "Sounds good," she said, but her smile didn't quite reach her eyes.

Gil turned to the round-faced man wearing glasses. "This is Harold Apfelbach," Gil added. "He's a photographer from Melbourne, here to get some shots of the local wildlife."

"Since I live in the city, I usually do portraits, cityscapes, that kind of thing. But every once in a while I get an assignment that takes me into the bush," Harold said. Judging by Harold's new-looking hiking clothes, Joe guessed that it was every once in a *long* while. "Had this specially made for the job," Harold added, patting the large aluminum case hanging from his shoulder by a strap, "to protect my equipment from the dust and rain."

Joe mumbled a greeting to Harold, but his mind was elsewhere. "I want to check out this guy Tracker before we head into the park," he told Gil.

"Tracker Jordan. His sheep station is over an hour's drive from here," Gil said. "I wouldn't go now, though. It'll be dark soon, and it's too dangerous to head out into the bush at night."

Joe hated putting off their investigation. But then he caught another look at Daphne. He wouldn't mind spending the evening getting to know her better. Now that he thought about it, he didn't mind taking the evening off at all.

"Wake up, sleepyhead."

Nancy heard George's voice floating toward her as if from a great distance. "Hmm?" She cracked open one eye and saw George grinning down at her. Sunshine streamed through the windows of their trailer. George was already up and dressed, and she was holding two mugs.

Nancy rubbed her eyes and sat up on the narrow bed. "I hope that's coffee," she said, sniffing the air, "because I've got a serious case of jet lag."

"This will help," George said with a laugh. "I made toast, too." She pointed to a plate on the table in the compact kitchen area. "Nellie's trailer isn't huge, but it has all the essentials."

Nancy got out of bed, washed her face in the tiny

bathroom, then pulled on jeans and a white tank top. As she sat across from George, she could see out the window to Mick's orange nylon tent pitched beneath a gum tree.

"So what's on the agenda for today, Nan?" George asked, taking a bite of toast. "Should we check out the Royces' mining office?"

"Definitely." Nancy took a sip of coffee, then said, "If they have the tjuringa, their office seems like a good place to start. Maybe Mick can—"

"Did I hear my name?" Mick asked, appearing outside their trailer window. His T-shirt was wrinkled and his blond hair slightly messed up, but somehow he looked cuter than ever to Nancy. She couldn't help grinning at him.

"Hey, Devlin," she called. "Come on in. George and I are just figuring out how to investigate Ian and Marian Royce."

Mick seemed to fill up the entire caravan. When he sat down next to Nancy, his arm brushed against hers, and she felt a tingle go up her spine. She had to force herself to concentrate on the case. "Maybe you and George can distract the Royces so I can look around." She pressed her lips together, thinking. "We'd better go without Nellie. If the Royces see her, they'll get suspicious."

"Good enough," Mick agreed. "Flat Hill is only a twenty-minute walk from here. We can go on foot."

After finishing their breakfast, the three of them started walking toward Flat Hill. Nellie's trailer was parked down a curving dirt road from her grandfather's house. It was before nine o'clock, but Nancy already felt perspiration on her forehead.

They were passing a low, wooden building, when Nancy got the distinct impression that someone was watching her. Looking through the building's wide windows, she saw rows of empty desks and a chalkboard, but the schoolhouse seemed empty.

A rippling metallic sound from above made her look up. A squat man with dark skin and a bushy mustache was standing on the roof of the building. He was holding a piece of corrugated aluminum. Apparently, he was repairing the roof, but his attention didn't seem to be on his work.

"Why is he glaring at us?" George whispered in Nancy's ear, glancing up at the man.

"Beats me," Nancy whispered back. The man's intense gaze was very unsettling.

"I'm pretty sure I've met him," Mick said, glancing at the man. "G'day!" he called out. "Didn't we meet at Nellie Mabo's?"

The man didn't answer. He slammed the piece of corrugated aluminum down noisily on the roof and began hammering it in place.

"Yami!" Mick said suddenly, snapping his fingers. "Yami Whiteair—that's your name. I'm sure we've met."

The man stopped hammering and peered down at Mick. "Don't talk to me," Yami said in a slow, angry voice. "Yungis' business is not your business."

"We're not trying to cause trouble. Nellie and her grandfather asked us to help," Mick explained.

That didn't seem to impress Yami. "Nellie Mabo is losing her Yungi spirit," he said. "She talks to you. She talks to people from the government. The government has given us only trouble." Yami shook his head disgustedly. "Aborigines must take what is ours. That is the only way to get what we deserve."

"Let's go," Nancy said softly to George and Mick.

They were almost past the schoolhouse when something caught Nancy's attention. The sun glinted off a pile of corrugated aluminum stacked next to the building, but she thought she saw a dark shape between two of the metal sheets. She paused, staring at it.

"Doesn't that look like a piece of wood?" she asked, pointing at the object.

George peered at the metal sheets, then frowned. "It's hard to tell from here."

Nancy jogged the dozen feet to the pile of roofing materials. It *was* a piece of wood. One flat end, about ten inches across, was sticking out from the metal. The wood was burnished with age, and it glistened, as if it had been carefully maintained. Nancy held her breath. Could it be . . . ?

As she bent over the board, she saw carved lines, circles, and dots covering it. She was still examining the symbols when Mick and George came up.

"I don't believe it!" Mick said, drawing in his breath sharply. "I think we've found the tjuringa!"

Chapter

Four

NANCY GENTLY PULLED the board from the pile of corrugated metal and held it up. The plaque was three feet long and covered with carved symbols. She, Mick, and George all stared at the board in amazement.

"It's beautiful," Mick said, "but I'm sure Nellie and her grandfather would have searched here. I wonder why they didn't—"

He broke off and turned toward a clump of bushes just behind the pile of corrugated aluminum. "Did you hear that?"

Nancy had heard the rustling noises, too. "Someone's back there!" She had taken only a few steps when she spotted a little girl peeking out at them from behind the bushes. Her fearful round eyes were focused on the tjuringa in Nancy's hands.

George had seen her, too. "She can't be older than five," she whispered. "Do you think she knows anything about this?"

"Let's find out," Nancy said. She crouched down and smiled at the little girl. "Hi, there," she said gently.

The little girl's eyes widened, and she jumped back behind the bushes. Nancy saw a flash of yellow shirt as the girl dashed toward the back of the schoolhouse. Then a high-pitched squeal rang in the air, followed by someone speaking. A second later Yami emerged from behind the schoolhouse, carrying the girl. Nancy noticed that Yami's demeanor had softened. He spoke to the little girl in a gentle voice. She hid her face in his shoulder as he came over to Nancy, Mick, and George.

"Jemma has brought the tjuringa back to us," Yami said. Holding the girl in one arm, he reached with his free hand and took the board from Nancy. "You are not a Yungi. You must not touch the tjuringa," he said, glowering at her.

Nancy remembered Mick saying something about that, but she had so many questions—she couldn't just walk away. "She had the board?" Nancy asked, nodding at the little girl. "But why did she take it? Where was she keeping it?"

"It is not your affair," Yami answered. "Come, Jemma. We will return this to its keeper."

That had to be Nellie's grandfather, Nancy realized. Shrugging at Mick, she said, "Let's wait in

Nellie's caravan. She can tell us what happened after she and her grandfather get all the details."

"You mean, that little girl was just playing with the tjuringa?" George stared at Nellie across the tiny table in Nellie's caravan an hour later.

"That's right," Nellie answered. She readjusted the knot of the red tie-dyed scarf she wore around her dark hair. "Last week Granddad showed the tjuringa to the children of the tribe and told them the story of the Honey Ant Father's dreaming," she explained. "Jemma asked to hear the story over and over, and she cried when Granddad put the tjuringa away. She was afraid that if it was out of her sight, the Honey Ant Father's path would be lost forever."

Nancy shook her head in amazement. "So she decided to take the board so that she could keep watch over the Honey Ant Father's path?"

Nellie nodded, then said, "She's so little. She didn't fully understand how important the tjuringa is until she saw everyone's reaction when the sacred board was gone. By then she was too scared to admit what she had done. She kept it hidden in her house until this morning, when she took it to the school. She knew someone would find it there and return it to Granddad."

"It looks as if you didn't need George and me after all," Nancy said, chuckling. "If we hadn't been around, someone else would have found the tjuringa soon. This case practically solved itself."

"Still, Granddad and I are thankful to you for

coming so far," Nellie said. She smiled at Nancy and George. "You can have a bit of a holiday now. I know I will celebrate tonight with my people."

"This is great!" George said, grinning across the table at Nancy and Mick. "The case is closed, and we're in the middle of the gorgeous Australian outback with time on our hands. What should we do?"

Nancy turned to Mick. "Any suggestions?" she asked.

"The outback is untamed. It's full of passion," he said. His green eyes flashed as they locked on Nancy. "The possibilities are endless."

Suddenly Nancy had the feeling that he wasn't just talking about the landscape. She nervously plucked at the fabric of her tank top. "Didn't Frank and Joe say they were going on a camping trip in Comet Creek National Park? I'm sure they wouldn't mind if we went along."

Mick acted disappointed, but all he said was, "Sounds good to me."

"Awesome!" George exclaimed. "Let's head over to Outback Adventures. Maybe we'll catch them before they leave."

"I can't believe these gorges are right near the dry, dusty outback," Frank commented later that afternoon.

Their path wound alongside the babbling waters of Comet Creek, while steep walls of white lime-stone rose impressively on either side of them.

Harold Apfelbach stopped next to Frank and

snapped a photograph of a bird that was such a bright blue Frank thought it would probably glow in the dark. "Blue wren," Harold explained. "I read up on the wildlife here before leaving Melbourne, but it's even more spectacular than I expected."

"Mmm," Frank said.

"You must think all Australians are like the blokes you see in the movies—killing crocs with their bare hands," Harold went on. "But the outback is as much of an adventure for me as it is for you."

Harold had been sticking close to Frank all day, but Frank didn't want to get caught up in a conversation with him. It would take his attention away from the case. He hadn't spotted any signs of poaching so far, but he was staying alert. *Someone* had to.

Joe was too busy trying to impress Daphne and hadn't noticed much of anything. He had started the night before, when Daphne and Harold had joined the group for dinner at the Flat Hill Lodge. Joe had dredged up every anecdote he could think of to show what an irresistible, macho guy he was, but Daphne hadn't seemed very impressed. It didn't look to Frank as if Joe was having any better luck now. Daphne had spent more time talking to George than to Joe.

Up ahead, Daphne paused next to an acacia bush and dug among its roots. "There's a witchetty grub," she said, as George and Joe bent over for a closer look. "If you're ever out in the bush with nothing to eat, they're a great source of protein. Many Aborigines consider them a delicacy."

"I think I'll pass for the moment," George said, grimacing at the wrinkled worm.

"Me, too," Joe put in. He turned to Daphne as the three of them continued down the trail. "Did I tell you about the time Frank and I were on a case in the Colorado Rockies?" he asked.

"Only thirty or forty times," Daphne said dryly, and went back to talking to George. Joe wasn't put off. While he butted in with another comment, Frank tuned them out and glanced behind him and Harold. Nancy and Mick were walking side by side about ten feet back. They hadn't said much since they'd set out. Frank wasn't sure what was going on between the two of them, but there was something about the way they gazed at each other. . . .

Daphne's irritated voice interrupted Frank's thoughts. "Joe, would you mind stopping your amazing outdoorsman act?" she was saying. "George and I are trying to have a conversation."

"Act?" Joe echoed. "For your information, I've done a lot of hiking and camping. Frank and I—" He broke off as his boot slipped on a mossy rock, and he stumbled.

"Oh, yes," Daphne said. "Your abilities in the outdoors are dazzling, Joe."

Harold gave Frank an uneasy glance. "Uh-oh," he said under his breath. "Looks like this could be a long day."

* * *

"Do you think those two are ever going to let up on each other?" Mick whispered to Nancy that night. The orange glow from the campfire reflected off his face as he nodded toward Daphne and Joe, who were sitting on the far side of the stone fireplace. The fireplaces existed at campsites throughout the park to help prevent bush fires, Daphne had explained. The group had taken great care while cooking to make sure no spark lit the dry leaves and branches on the floor of the gorge.

"Beats me," Nancy answered. "Joe can be pretty stubborn."

"Especially when he's around a girl who knows more about the wilderness and camping than he does," George put in, keeping her voice low. She finished stowing their clean camp pots in her pack, then squatted on her heels next to Nancy.

"They've been on each other's case about how to pitch a tent, how to build a campfire, even how to roast marshmallows," Mick said, shaking his head. "I don't know how much more I can take."

Apparently, the others felt the same way. Harold had retreated to his tent right after dinner. Soon after, Frank had gone to the tent he and Joe were sharing. Now George pulled a small book from her back pocket and held it so that the fire illuminated the pages. "It's a guide to the park," she explained. "Daphne lent it to me."

"Hey! I don't have to take any flak from a bloke who's got an ego bigger than all of Queensland!" Daphne's voice rose, catching Nancy's attention.

Joe rolled his eyes at Daphne, then continued roasting his marshmallow. *"My* ego? *I'm* not the one who's pretending to be some kind of female Tarzan of the Australian bush."

Mick let out a low groan. Leaning close to Nancy, he whispered, "Those two aren't making it easy for the rest of us to appreciate Comet Creek. Care to take a walk?"

"Good idea." Nancy got to her feet, then hesitated as she took in the black shadows surrounding the clearing where their camp was. "I guess it's okay, as long as we don't go too far."

"I'll bring a flashlight, and we can stick to the riverbank so we won't get lost," Mick said.

As Nancy and Mick moved farther away from the campsite, Joe's and Daphne's voices were gradually replaced by the soft babbling of the creek and the rustling of night animals. For several minutes Nancy and Mick walked without saying anything.

"I feel as if we're a million miles from civilization," Nancy finally whispered. A sudden squawking in a nearby tree made her raise her eyes to the black, shadowy web of branches. "It's almost as if the animals are warning one another about us."

Mick chuckled. "Australia is full of unusual animals, but out here, I guess *we're* the oddities."

As they continued walking, a mood of happy contentment fell over Nancy. "It's so beautiful here," she whispered.

Mick stopped and turned to her. "The scenery is nothing compared to the company."

He took her hand, and Nancy could feel her heart start to beat faster. "Mick . . . I don't know if . . . I mean, I thought we already decided—"

"Shh." He gently pressed a finger to her lips. "That's in the past," he said softly. "Let's forget all that and concentrate on the present."

Nancy could feel herself being drawn to him, to his warmth and gentleness. She hadn't expected this to happen. "Mick, when I came here I didn't plan on—"

"I didn't plan it, either," he interrupted gently. "But when I saw you at the airport, I realized that I still have feelings for you." He put his hands on her shoulders. "Strong feelings."

All of a sudden, Nancy knew he was going to kiss her. As he bent his head closer to hers, she closed her eyes. . . .

Cra-aack!

Nancy's eyes popped open, and she jumped back with a gasp. "Mick! That was a rifle shot!"

Chapter

Five

INSTINCTIVELY JOE JUMPED to his feet, then crouched behind the stone fireplace.

"Whoa!" George dropped her book and fell to the ground. "What was that!"

"What's going on?" "That was a shot!" "Is everyone okay out there?"

Confused voices rang out, but Joe kept his attention focused on the trees to his left, where the rifle shot had come from. All of his senses were alert as he stared into the darkness.

The rustle of someone running through the brush jolted him into action. "Frank! I'm going after the shooter!" Joe called over his shoulder. He took off into the darkness at top speed, blinking to help his eyes adjust to the dark. He couldn't take the time to get his flashlight—by then the shooter would be gone. Tree branches whipped at his arms and legs, but he hardly noticed them. All he was aware of were the crashing noises of the person ahead of him. Joe just hoped whoever it was was too busy running to think about using the rifle again.

"George and I are behind you!" Frank called.

"Mick and I are here, too," Nancy's voice came from farther back.

Just then Joe heard a loud crash up ahead, followed by a muffled "Ouch!" as if the person had fallen. Joe picked up his pace.

"Hey! Who's there?" It was Daphne's voice. It sounded as if she were ahead of him, near the person he was chasing. The others' voices echoed around him, making it hard to tell where everyone was.

Joe paused to get his bearings, then ran forward around a bush when he spotted a dark silhouette beyond it. He was getting closer now. . . .

"Ooomph!" The breath was knocked out of him as someone slammed into him from the side. The next thing he knew, he was on the ground and pinned down.

"Hey! What—?" Joe managed to get his arms around the person's torso. Gritting his teeth, he flipped the person off him, then pinned the person's arms behind his back. He was gulping for air as he bent to get a look at the person's face.

"Harold?" Even in the darkness, Joe could see the scared expression on the photographer's face. Harold's glasses were twisted, and one round cheek was jammed into the ground. *"You're* the poacher?"

"N-no!" Harold stammered. "I have special night film. I couldn't sleep so I decided to take some photos. Then someone shot at me!" Harold's whole body was shaking.

Joe let go of Harold and stared into the darkness, his entire body tense. "If the poacher is going from animal targets to human ones, we could be in serious trouble. Are you sure he was shooting—"

Joe heard someone running through the brush from the same direction Harold had come from. He whipped around and dropped to a crouch. Seconds later Daphne appeared, flashlight in hand. She stopped short when she saw Joe and Harold. "Where's the poacher? I thought I saw someone."

"We both did," Joe said. He cocked his head, listening. All he heard were the voices of their party. There were no sounds of anyone running through the brush. "Whoever it was got away," he said, banging his fist into his palm.

Harold was sitting up now. He reached for his camera case, then got to his feet and pushed his glasses into place. "I don't know, maybe we were all just chasing one another," he said, shaking his head.

Joe clenched his teeth and glared at Daphne. "Hmm. Maybe that's exactly what we were doing." An idea had just occurred to him, but before he could explore it, Daphne turned back toward the camp, lighting the way with her flashlight.

"Look, I'm sorry I ran into you," Harold told

Joe. He reached into the pocket of his nylon jacket, pulled out a flashlight, and handed it to Joe. "This should help."

Joe took the flashlight and turned it on, then started back toward the camp. He kept an eye on Daphne's beam ahead and flicked his own flashlight around, checking for evidence. He and Harold had gone only a few yards when Frank called urgently, "Joe! Over here."

Joe found his brother, George, Mick, and Daphne about fifty paces from camp. They were bent over a furry lump on the ground, while Nancy paced the surrounding area. When he played his flashlight over the animal, Joe saw that the yellowish fur on its upturned stomach was stained with fresh blood. It looked something like an opossum —and it was very dead.

"That's a yellow-bellied night glider," Daphne said, gazing soberly at the animal. "It's a marsupial, like a kangaroo. Those furry flaps attached to its legs allow it to glide from tree to tree."

"Not anymore," Frank said grimly.

Nancy stepped out from a bush several feet away. She was dragging a sheet of heavy plastic about four feet square. "I found this under that bush," she said. "I'm beginning to see a pattern here."

"Looks that way," George said. "Gil said he found plastic near the dead bettong. But I didn't see a hole where the poacher could bury the glider to keep the remains safe from other wild animals."

"I doubt the shooter had enough time to dig

one. . . ." Frank's voice trailed off as his flashlight beam glinted off something small and metallic on the ground near the bush Nancy had pointed out. As he jogged over to it, he realized that it was the casing from a rifle shell.

"Find something?" Nancy asked. Frank looked over his shoulder to see her frowning down at the bullet casing. "Small, silver . . . What do you want to bet it comes from a custom-made rifle?"

"Probably," Frank agreed. "We can check with park security when we leave the gorges." Straightening up, he turned to look for his brother. Daphne, George, and Mick were still bent over the night glider, but Joe wasn't with them.

Joe pushed through some bushes next to Frank and Nancy right then. He had Harold's flashlight in one hand, and in the other a knife. He had wrapped a large leaf around the handle so that he wouldn't get his prints on it. "Looks as if the poacher dropped this."

Frank peered more closely. The sturdy, pointed blade had been carefully maintained, and the red leather handle was shiny from use. Despite the distinctive swirls that were tooled into the leather, Frank had a feeling that this knife was used for a lot more than just decoration. "I wonder why the poacher would have this? There aren't any knife cuts in the glider."

"Maybe the person wanted to skin the animal, but with us chasing, there wasn't time to do it," Nancy said.

"Could be," Joe agreed. He took a few steps toward the others and held out the knife. "Any of you recognize this?"

George, Harold, and Mick all shook their heads, but Frank saw Daphne's eyes narrow. She hesitated as she brushed a hand through her auburn hair. Finally, she, too, shook her head. "Sorry."

A moment later Joe took Frank aside and whispered, "I don't buy Daphne's innocent act," he said in a low voice.

"She does seem nervous about the knife," Frank said. "But I don't see her as a poacher. I mean, she seems to have total respect for nature."

Joe frowned. "All I know is that right before the shots, Daphne got really mad at me."

"No," Frank said sarcastically. "Was it something you said?"

"Very funny," Joe said. "Anyway, she stormed away from the camp, and the next thing I know, someone is shooting that night glider. Not only that, but I'm almost sure I heard her voice come from the same direction as the shot." He raised an eyebrow at Frank. "Kind of makes me think that maybe she was the person I was chasing."

"She left the camp?" Frank glanced at Daphne, who was using a stone to dig a shallow grave for the night glider. "I don't know. Maybe she knows more than she's admitting, but we still don't have any concrete evidence. Or a motive. If you ask me, Dennis Moore is the more likely suspect. From what Regina Bourke said, trafficking in poached rare animals is a way of life for him."

"True," Joe conceded. "When we get back to Flat Hill, we'll have to find out from Gil if he was able to track Moore's movements. I'm not dropping Daphne as a suspect, though. For all we know, she'd kill an animal right under our noses, just to prove that she could get away with it."

The sound of a snapping twig made Frank shine his flashlight to the left. George was a few feet from him and Joe, her expression troubled. "You guys actually believe *Daphne* killed that night glider?"

"Shh!" Frank shot a quick look at Daphne, but she didn't appear to have heard George. "We don't know anything for sure," he hedged.

"But she is a suspect, so keep an eye on her, okay?" Joe added.

Planting her hands on her hips, George faced off with Joe. "You mean, spy on her? Forget it!" she whispered angrily. "You're way off base, Joe. You can't stand the idea that Daphne knows more about surviving in the outdoors than you do. That's why you're accusing her. You're jealous."

"Hey, cool it!" Frank said, stepping between Joe and George. "You two are friends, remember?"

"I used to think so," George said. Then she turned around and walked back to Daphne.

Frank let out his breath in a rush. "Whether or not Daphne's the poacher, I think we should keep an eye on things tonight," he whispered to Joe. "You, Nancy, and I can take turns keeping watch. I just hope the poacher doesn't decide to strike again."

* * *

"Can you believe that this rock painting has been here for ten thousand years?" George said the next morning.

"Give or take a few thousand," Daphne added with a laugh. "Aborigines lived in this gorge as far back as nineteen thousand years ago."

Joe stifled a yawn as he stared at the pictures that covered the walls of the limestone cave they were in. Keeping watch the night before had cut into his sleeping time, but at least the poacher hadn't struck again. Joe promised himself not to let Daphne distract him with any arguments. Daphne and George took the lead as they left the cave, so Joe dropped back behind Frank, Mick, and Harold to put distance between them.

"Are you and George planning on ever talking to each other again, Joe?" Nancy asked.

"I feel bad about that," he admitted. He slowed, waiting until Harold was out of earshot, then said in a low voice, "I know I can be hotheaded, but Daphne *is* a suspect in the poaching. She left camp right before the shooting, and I'm sure she recognized the knife we found near the night glider."

Nancy gave a sober nod. "Maybe if you try talking to George again, you can get her to see that there are sound reasons for suspecting Daphne."

"I'd like to, but she and Daphne have gotten so chummy that I haven't had a chance."

The cave was set into one of the limestone cliffs, about fifteen feet above the floor of the gorge. As they went single-file down a log ramp, Joe fell quiet, thinking about the previous night's poaching. It wasn't until he heard the sound of crashing water that he became aware of his surroundings. Checking his watch, he saw that it was nearly noon.

"There's a gorgeous waterfall up ahead," Daphne said. "We can stop for a breather there."

When the waterfall came into view, Nancy pulled up short in front of Joe. "Wow!"

It was amazing, Joe had to admit. Water cascaded from a cliff hundreds of feet above them, spilling into a wide pool at their feet. The rock walls on either side of the falls dripped with water and were covered with lush mosses, ferns, and orchids. The steep slopes leading up the gorge were so overgrown with gum trees and tree ferns that Joe couldn't even see the ground beneath.

"Where does that trail go?" Mick asked. He pointed to a steep path that disappeared into the dense foliage.

"To the top of the gorge," Daphne answered, dropping her pack to the ground. "It's rough going, though, since it runs right next to the waterfall." She stared straight at Joe, a challenging look in her gray eyes. "I don't recommend it for anyone who's not an expert bush walker."

"No problem," Joe said, staring back at her. "Anyone else want to come?"

"Count me in," Frank said.

"I'm game," Nancy added. "How about you guys?" she asked Mick and George.

Mick gave a thumbs-up sign, but George shook

her head. "I want to see if I can find some of the edible plants Daphne's been telling me about."

Harold took one look up the steep slope and shook his head. "Thanks, but I want to photograph the falls," he said, patting his camera case.

"There's a main path that angles up gently to the top of the gorge," Daphne said, pointing to a second path, which led into the trees farther away from the waterfall. "Harold, George, and I will take that one. It meets up with the waterfall path at the top of the gorge. Just look for the white trail marker and wait for us there."

"Like I said, no problem," Joe told her. After readjusting his pack, he started up the waterfall trail at a fast clip. Following the blue trail markers, he was glad for the chance to burn off some steam. After just a few minutes, he saw that he was well ahead of the others.

"I'll meet you at the top," he called back as he grabbed a root and pulled himself around a small boulder. The trail followed a difficult zigzag path. Before long Joe was sweating and breathing hard. The tree ferns were so overgrown that he couldn't see the clearing where they'd left Daphne, George, and Harold. The sound of the water drowned out any voices. Joe felt as if he had the whole park to himself.

About halfway up the cliff, the path leveled out to a rock ledge that overlooked the waterfall. "Not bad," Joe murmured to himself, taking in the view of the tumbling falls and the pool of water far below. Closing his eyes, he breathed in the cool, moist air.

Joe heard a rustle in the bushes a split second before he felt two hands against his back.

"Hey!" he cried, but the sound was choked off as he flew forward. The next thing he knew, he was toppling over the rock ledge!

Chapter

Six

J OE FELT HIS STOMACH shoot into his throat as he
plummeted downward. In one dizzying glance, he
saw the rushing waterfall and the rocks and trees
far below. He grasped frantically at the rocks, but
his hands ripped through the moss and flowers.

"Nooo!"

One hand hit a sapling growing out of the side of
the cliff, and he made a wild grab for it. His fingers
curled around the small trunk, and he gripped it as
tightly as he could with both hands. He had managed to stop his fall, but his arms felt as if they were
being ripped right out of his shoulder sockets. He
winced from the pain as he dangled in midair.

"Joe! Are you all right? What happened?"
Frank's anxious voice came from above.

Angling his head back, Joe saw his brother,

Nancy, and Mick staring down at him from the rock shelf. "I think so," Joe called up. "You guys, someone pu—

"Whoa!"

The tree he was holding on to gave a little, and he dropped another half foot. Pebbles and dirt rained down on him. "Get me out of here!" he yelled.

"Don't move, Joe," Nancy called out.

Joe didn't dare look at them anymore, but he could hear his brother, Nancy, and Mick talking in low voices. "I'm coming down, Joe," Frank said after a few moments. "Mick and Nancy are going to lower me by my feet. Once I've got your wrists, they'll pull us both back up again."

The tree gave some more, scattering more rocks and earth. "Just hurry!" Joe muttered through clenched teeth. He tried not to think about the searing pain in his shoulders and concentrated on not budging. He hardly let himself breathe. After a few moments he felt more pebbles and heard a scraping noise against the rocks overhead.

"I'm almost to you, Joe," Frank said. "Nancy, Mick, a little lower."

Joe heard Frank's gasp and the ripping noise of the tree at the same time. He started to drop again, but this time Frank's hands closed firmly around his wrists.

"I've got him!" Frank called.

When they were finally on the ledge again, Joe and Frank fell back against the rocks, gulping for air. "Are you all right?" Frank asked between breaths.

Joe sat up and slowly rubbed each shoulder. "Yeah, I think so," he replied. "Thanks, guys."

"Glad to be of service," Nancy said with a grin.

Mick gazed out over the edge of the narrow rock shelf. "I guess Daphne was right about the difficulty of this trail," he said.

"Difficult, nothing," Joe retorted. "Someone pushed me."

"What!" Frank, Nancy, and Mick all cried.

"I was pushed," Joe said again. "When I heard someone on the path, I thought it was one of you, but before I could turn around, the person decided to give me a flying lesson."

Frank frowned at his brother. "I didn't see anyone else, did you guys?" he asked Nancy and Mick. They shook their heads.

"Then how?" Nancy peered up and down the trail, then backtracked a few steps. "There's another trail over here," she called.

"But I thought Daphne said the main trail doesn't meet up with this one until after we get to the top of the gorge," Frank said, frowning. Pushing to his feet, he jogged over to Nancy. Sure enough, a small trail forked off, leading away from the waterfall trail. "This trail's marked with red," he said, pointing to the slash of bright paint on one of the tree trunks. "But our path is blue, and the main trail is marked with white."

"Looks as if someone took a detour," Joe said as he and Mick joined Nancy and Frank at the new trail. He examined the hard-packed earth for clues. "I don't see any footprints. The ground's too hard.

But someone knows the park well enough to maneuver to this spot and push me from that ledge."

"Someone from our group?" Mick asked.

"Daphne Whooten, for instance," Joe said soberly.

Nancy's brow was furrowed. "It could be someone outside our group who's been keeping track of our movements. That collector of animals must be used to sneaking around in the wild, if he deals in rare, protected species. Maybe he's been following us."

"Could be." In his mind, Frank flashed on the tanned, arrogant face of the sheep rancher who'd brought the dead kangaroo to the Flat Hill Lodge. "It's a long shot, but what about Tracker Jordan? We haven't seen any signs of him, but he would know his way around the bush."

"And he doesn't exactly have the greatest respect for the animals around here," Joe added. "When we get back to Flat Hill, let's make it our business to find out where Tracker and that collector have been these last twenty-four hours. But for right now, I want to find out what Daphne's been up to."

Frank was lost in thought as they hiked the rest of the way to the rendezvous point. He wasn't looking forward to telling Gil that his own employee was a suspect in the poachings and in the attack on Joe. Obviously, Nancy and George weren't even in the running as suspects. Mick hadn't arrived until after the poacher had already struck, and Harold didn't seem to have the know-how to hike and kill on his own in the bush. Daphne did.

The sound of voices told Frank that they had rendezvoused with the others. Daphne, George, and Harold were sitting cross-legged in the low, scrubby grass, looking at a map of the national park.

"What took you so long?" Daphne asked. "Was the trail tougher than you thought?"

Frank could see his brother's jaw tighten. "We would have gotten here sooner, but someone decided to show me the fast way *down* the gorge," Joe retorted. "By pushing me off a rock ledge."

George's jaw dropped open. "What!"

"You're kidding, right?" Harold said. He looked from Joe, to Frank, Nancy, and Mick. "No, you're not kidding. What's going on here?"

Frank noticed that Daphne didn't even seem to have heard Harold's question. "Pushed?" she echoed, staring at Joe. "Maybe you just slipped."

Joe's face turned red, and he balled his hands into fists at his sides. Frank was grateful when Nancy stepped in. "Do you mind if I look at that map?" she asked, putting down her pack.

She had to be thinking about the trail they'd found near the rock ledge where Joe fell, Frank thought. Looking over her shoulder, he saw her run her finger along the blue trail they had taken alongside the waterfall. Halfway up the waterfall, a squiggly red line branched off from the trail. It intersected with the main trail about three quarters of the way up the white trail's more roundabout path to the top of the gorge.

Frank saw the way Joe's jaw tightened as he

stared at the map. Shooting Daphne a hooded glance, Joe said, "Someone could have taken that trail, pushed me off the cliff, then raced back to the main trail."

"I hope you're not saying that one of us pushed you," Daphne said.

"If you were all together, then there's no reason to suspect anyone," Frank put in quickly.

"Actually, we each decided to take the path at our own speed," George said.

"I got here just a few minutes before you," Harold finished. "I was so busy taking photos that I lost track of time."

Frank watched closely while Harold unscrewed the telephoto lens from his camera, opened his aluminum carrying case, and exchanged the lens for a 35mm one. Frank spotted two lenses, film, and cleaning tissues set into custom niches in the case—nothing that resembled a rifle. Still, if Daphne or Harold was the poacher, one of them was keeping a rifle somewhere.

Frank's gaze moved to the packs stacked at the edge of the clearing. He caught Joe's eye, then gave an imperceptible nod toward the packs. Joe's answering nod told Frank he understood. Turning to Daphne, George, and Harold, Joe demanded, "Okay, who got here first?"

Daphne immediately lashed back with a defensive comment, and Harold and George jumped in with their own explanations. Frank saw that they were all too involved in the argument to pay any attention to him.

He walked over to the packs, dropped his own pack next to them, and pretended to search for something inside his. Then he reached for Daphne's red pack, quickly loosened the top flap, and poked his hand inside. He felt clothes, cans of food, and a small cloth bag of toiletries—no gun or rifle. Frank fastened the flap, then moved to Harold's pack. Groping around with his hand, he felt shirts, a towel, more supplies. Nothing suspicious there, either. He let out a sigh as he closed the flap. This case was growing more frustrating with every second. And more dangerous!

"I almost forgot how wide open and arid the outback is outside of Comet Creek," Nancy said Monday morning. She, George, Mick, and Harold were standing next to the national parks center at the entrance to Comet Creek National Park. They were in the shade of a stand of eucalyptus trees, but ahead of them the green landscape gave way to endless, dry tableland.

"It feels at least ten degrees hotter here," George commented, blowing some air under the dark curls on her forehead.

Harold nodded. "I hope Frank and Joe hurry up, so we can leave."

Just then Frank, Joe, and Daphne came out of the center. "We were right," Joe told Nancy. "The shell casing Frank found matches the one Gil turned over to the park officials last week. They recognized it right away."

"So it's definitely the same poacher," Harold

said with disgust. "Some people have no respect for nature."

"Well, at least the poacher didn't strike last night," Mick said, climbing into Daphne's Range Rover. Nancy and George got in with him, while Harold joined the Hardys in their rented Rover.

"We handed over the knife we found, but trying to track down a poacher in those gorges is impossible," Frank said. "We might as well let the park security people investigate since they know the turf better than we do. Meanwhile, Joe and I can follow leads back in Flat Hill."

They made the drive back to Flat Hill in silence. As they passed the airstrip outside the town, Nancy noticed someone bent over the open engine of a small propeller plane. "Is that Roger, the guy who flies the supply plane?" she asked.

Daphne squinted toward the airstrip. "No, it's Gil," she said. "Looks like he's got some kind of trouble." She pulled up to the strip and honked. The Hardys were right behind them. When Gil turned to look at them, Nancy saw the worry lines on his forehead.

"What's up, Gil?" Frank asked. He and Joe hopped from their Range Rover and jogged to the plane.

"Clogged fuel line," Gil answered, wiping his greasy hands on his pants. "I'm supposed to hop over to the Great Barrier Reef to pick up some clients who want to bush walk at Comet Creek. Doesn't look as if I'll be getting there any time soon, though." He shook his head. "I can't afford to lose business, because I had to take out a loan to keep Outback Adventures running. I need every penny I can scrape together to pay it off."

Turning back to the Range Rover, Joe said, "You guys go ahead. Frank and I will stay here to help Gil."

Gil started to object, then thought better of it. "Thanks. I appreciate it."

"I'll drop Harold off in town," Daphne offered. Harold climbed in with his pack. A few minutes later Daphne and Harold dropped off Nancy, Mick, and George at the entrance to the Yungi community.

"Boy, could I use a shower," George said as they shouldered their packs and started for the trailer.

Nancy nodded. "Me, too."

"While you shower, I'm going to see how Nellie's doing," Mick said.

The rest of what he said was drowned out by the loud engine of an approaching vehicle. A four-wheel-drive vehicle with two people in it roared into view. Nancy caught a glimpse of blond hair flying in the wind as the car screeched around them.

"Hey! Watch it," George yelled indignantly.

"Wasn't that Marian Royce?" Nancy asked.

"Yes. And her husband, Ian," Mick said. "I bet they're here to give Nellie more trouble."

He broke into a run, taking off after them. Hitching her pack up on her shoulders, Nancy ran after him. "Come on, George. We'd better go, too."

Nancy was breathless by the time they reached

Mr. Mabo's house. The Royces' four-wheel drive was parked next to Nellie's truck, and Ian and Marian were standing outside Mr. Mabo's front door. Nancy could see Nellie's grandfather framed in the open doorway.

"Let us in!" Marian demanded. "You can't protect Nellie, not after what she's done."

Mr. Mabo stared unflinchingly at her. "Nellie is not here," he said quietly.

"What's going on?" Mick demanded, running to the doorway. "Why are you bothering Mr. Mabo?"

Marian didn't look at all pleased to see him. "Not that it's any of your business," Marian said, tapping her shoe impatiently on the ground, "but we've been robbed."

"What was taken?" Nancy asked.

"Opals," Ian Royce said. "Someone broke into our safe during the night and stole a felt bag full of black opals. There were over fifty stones in all— worth a hundred and fifty thousand dollars!"

Mick dropped his pack to the ground and crossed his arms over his chest. "Sorry to hear that, but shouldn't you go to the police?"

"Don't you get it?" Marian huffed. "We came here because the thief is your friend Nellie Mabo."

Chapter

Seven

YOU'VE GOT TO BE KIDDING!" Mick burst out. "Nellie would never steal anything."

"Then how do you explain the fact that Ian found *this* inside our office?" Marian reached into her shoulder bag and pulled out a red scarf with tie-dyed yellow circles on it.

"That *is* Nellie's," George whispered to Nancy.

Nancy nodded. Glancing at Nellie's grandfather, she saw that his steady gaze was fixed on the scarf. "Where is Nellie, Mr. Mabo?" she asked.

"I'll tell you where she is," Marian interrupted. "She's on the run. Tracker Jordan saw her leave with Roger on this morning's supply run."

"That isn't possible," Mr. Mabo said slowly. "We're meeting our lawyer this afternoon. Nellie would not miss that."

"I'm afraid it's true," Ian Royce said. "We ran into Tracker right after we discovered the theft. He was driving in to pick up barbed wire and had seen Nellie at the airstrip."

Nancy had a hard time believing that Nellie would stoop to stealing. But she and her grandfather did feel strongly about the Yungis' land rights. Nancy couldn't ignore the possibility that Nellie had decided to take drastic measures. "Can you tell us where Nellie is, Mr. Mabo?" Nancy asked.

"She is not here" was all he said.

"This whole accusation is outrageous," Mick added. "How do we know the opals were really stolen? You two might have made up this whole story just to get Nellie off your backs." Nancy had never seen him so angry.

"Have a look for yourselves at the office," Ian said. "We've got to get back there ourselves to meet the police. We rang them over an hour ago, and it would take 'em about this long to get here from Roma."

"Everything takes forever in this uncivilized dump," Marian grumbled.

"We'll take you up on that offer," Mick said firmly. Turning to Nellie's grandfather, he asked, "Mr. Mabo, would you mind if we borrowed Nellie's truck?"

After the older man nodded, Ian gave them directions to the Royce mining office. "We'll meet you there," he said. Then he and Marian left.

George's expression was grim as they walked

over to Nellie's beat-up green pickup. "Looks as if we might be staying on a case, after all."

"From what we've heard so far, it's not good for Nellie," Nancy added. She and George put their backpacks in the truck bed, then got in the passenger side. Mick climbed into the driver's seat a few moments later. His jaw was clenched, and there was a dark expression in his eyes.

"I don't like this," he told Nancy and George. "Mr. Mabo just told me that Nellie left early this morning and hasn't been back since. It's not like her to take off without a word to anyone. He's worried, and so am I. I know she didn't take those opals, but something must have happened."

Nancy gave Mick's hand an encouraging squeeze. "Let's not jump to any conclusions," she told him.

The Royce Mining office was located in a plain brick building at the edge of Flat Hill. As Mick parked in front of the office, Nancy saw a few people in hiking clothes, but otherwise the street was quiet. It didn't seem likely that anyone would have been around at the crack of dawn to spot the thief.

A police car was parked in front of the office. "Morning, Lou," Ian greeted the officer.

The man who got out of the car was over six feet tall. He wore a khaki uniform, and there was a serious expression on his rugged face. "G'day, Ian, Marian," he said, lifting his hat slightly. "Hear you've got some trouble."

When Mick, Nancy, and George joined the

group, Marian and Ian introduced the man as Officer Downs. They told the officer their story as they unlocked the office door and went inside. The front room of Royce Mining was a showroom. Framed photographs of digging equipment, mine shafts, and machines used to process opals decorated the walls. A glass display case held samples of the luminous stones, which glinted with fiery specks of color. Nancy wished she and George could see more, but Marian and Ian led them and Officer Downs through a doorway and into another room.

"The safe is in the office, back here," Marian was explaining.

George stopped short just inside the door. "What a mess!"

A feeling of dread settled over Nancy as she took in the scene. Framed pictures had been knocked off the walls, leaving broken glass everywhere. Papers were scattered on the floor, and two straight-backed chairs had been knocked over.

"Looks as if the thief decided to rough things up a bit while he was at it," said Officer Downs.

"While *she* was at it, you mean," Marian insisted. "We all know the thief is Nellie Mabo."

"Speak for yourself," George muttered.

Officer Downs didn't comment. Nancy followed him over to the safe, which was set into the wall above the metal desk. She saw that the dial was cracked, and the locking mechanism was completely shattered.

Officer Downs let out a low whistle. "It's hard to do that much damage to a safe," he said.

"Unless you use liquid nitrogen," Nancy put in. She knew from other cases she'd worked on that liquid nitrogen had the ability to freeze metal and make it brittle. "The thief could have poured it into the locking mechanism. After that, all it takes is one tap of a hammer and the whole thing shatters."

"Right you are," Officer Downs said, obviously surprised by Nancy's knowledge.

"We found the scarf right here," Ian said, pointing to the floor beneath the safe.

"Nancy," Mick said from across the room. He and George were bent over some broken glass. "See that?"

Hurrying over to them, Nancy saw some dried, reddish brown splotches on the glass. "Blood," she said. "The question is, whose is it?"

"Nellie's, of course," Marian said impatiently. "She must have cut herself while she was demolishing the place."

"I don't get it," George said, staring around the office. "Why did the thief make such a mess? That safe is in plain view."

Nancy had been thinking the same thing. "Maybe there was a fight."

"I'll check into all possibilities," Officer Downs said. Turning to Nancy, Mick, and George, he added, "I'm afraid you'll have to leave. I want to keep the crime scene clear until I'm through here."

Nancy wished they could stay, but Officer Downs was already ushering them out of the office. As soon as they were outside, Mick exploded. "What if that is Nellie's blood on that glass?" he asked. "She could be hurt."

"That makes it even more important to find out where she went and why she's on the run," Nancy said. "My gut feeling is that she wouldn't steal anything from anyone. But there was definitely a fight in that office. Either Nellie found the thief—"

"Or someone planted her scarf there to make it look as if she stole the opals," George finished.

"Either way, Nellie's in trouble, and I've got to try to clear her," Mick said firmly. "I know you two already accomplished what you came here for, but—"

"We'll do everything we can to help," Nancy offered without hesitating.

"Definitely," George agreed. "Anyway, I wouldn't be able to have fun knowing Nellie's in trouble."

Mick smiled wearily. "Thanks."

Nancy's mind was already racing ahead to their next step. "Is there any way to find out where Roger was flying to this morning?" she asked Mick.

"He makes regular runs to Brisbane and Sydney," Mick said. "Let's try asking at the Flat Hill Lodge. Roger flies in most of their supplies."

After driving to the inn, Nancy and George waited in the lobby while Mick spoke to Regina in the restaurant.

"We're in luck," he said, returning with a slip of paper in his hand. "Regina says the supply plane was headed for Brisbane." He strode over to the pay phone. "There's a phone at the cargo hangar Roger uses in Brisbane." He pulled a handful of change from his pocket, pumped several coins into the phone, and dialed.

"Hello. Roger, is that you?" Mick spoke into the receiver. "Great! Listen, is Nellie Mabo with you? I've got to speak with her."

As he listened, Mick's expression darkened. "Yeah. . . . Airlie, eh? . . . The police? . . . Yes, that's why I'm calling, too." He let out a long sigh, then said, "Thanks just the same, Roger. 'Bye."

Even without hearing the other end of the conversation, Nancy knew the news wasn't good. "She already left?" she guessed.

Mick nodded. "Roger says he heard her calling information about buses to Airlie Beach. That's up the coast from Brisbane." He frowned. "From there, who knows where she'll go—maybe out to one of the Whitsundays."

"The whats?" George asked.

"Sorry," Mick said. "The Whitsunday Islands. They're at the southern edge of the Great Barrier Reef, in the Coral Sea north of Brisbane."

"Did I hear you say something about the police?" Nancy asked Mick. "Are they trying to track her down, too?"

"Yeah. The police there have already questioned Roger. Told him they want to ask her about the stolen opals. I don't know how I'm going to do it, but I've got to find her." Mick raked a hand through his blond hair and looked at Nancy and

George. "How about a trip to Australia's famous Great Barrier Reef?"

Nancy grinned at him. "I thought you'd never ask. If we hurry, maybe we can catch Gil before he leaves."

"Um, you guys?" George hesitated. "What about our other suspects? I mean, maybe I should stick around here and follow up on the Royces. You know, see if I can find anything to show that they're setting up Nellie."

Nancy hated leaving George behind, but her idea made sense. "If we can find the real opal thief, that will help clear Nellie," she agreed. "Are you sure you don't mind staying here on your own?"

"No problem," George told her. "The Hardys are here. We can help each other while you're gone. Daphne can probably help, too."

"In that case," Nancy turned to Mick with a grin, "let's go!"

Frank stared after Gil's plane as it took off from the airstrip. In the distance, a group of kangaroos scattered, bounding among the scrub. As the noise from the droning engine faded, Frank turned to his brother and said, "I guess it was a good thing that it took so long to get that fuel line fixed. Otherwise Nancy and Mick would have missed getting a ride to the coast. I wish we could do more to help, but until we solve our case and find whoever's been poaching . . ." Frank shrugged.

"I'd love to check out Dennis Moore, but you

heard Gil. Moore left Flat Hill this morning to go visit the Yungis and another aboriginal settlement in the outback," Joe said with a frown.

"His import-export business sounds to me like a cover for poaching," Frank said. "Too bad Gil got that call from his clients and couldn't follow Moore. But remember that Gil said Moore was in Flat Rock the whole time we were in Comet Creek, so he couldn't have shot the night glider or pushed you."

"He could be paying someone else to do the poaching for him," Joe pointed out. "Which brings us back to Daphne Whooten or Tracker Jordan. We haven't had a chance to check out Jordan, and it's only one o'clock. We could go out to his sheep station and be back long before dark."

Frank's stomach growled, reminding him that he hadn't eaten since before hiking out of Comet Creek early that morning. "Fine, but first we eat lunch. And take showers." He hoisted his pack over one shoulder by the straps, then wiped his greasy hands on his pants. "I don't know about you, but I feel as if I've been wearing these clothes for a week."

A hot wind whipped over Frank's face and arms as their Range Rover bounced over the dusty road. When they reached the paved road at the edge of town, Joe suddenly slowed down.

"Look who's there," Joe said, pointing.

Up ahead, Frank spotted Daphne's white Rover. Her red-brown hair flew out behind her as she roared away from a wooden house at the end of Flat Hill's main street.

"That must be where she lives." As soon as the words were out of his mouth, Frank realized what his brother was thinking. "Feel like taking a detour to search her place?"

"It's the only way we can find out whether she's got a custom rifle," Joe answered. "Or the carcasses or skins of any animals she's killed."

"What an appetizing thought," Frank said, grimacing. "Okay, let's go."

Daphne had already disappeared down the street, so Joe pulled up to her house and he and Frank hopped out. Frank knocked, and when there was no answer, he turned the front doorknob.

"It's open," he said, grinning. "I guess security isn't a top priority here." He pushed open the door and stepped into the living room. The wooden furniture looked as if it had been made by local craftspeople. The rug and the throw pillows on the couch echoed the browns, yellows, and oranges of the outback. Frank saw the kitchen stove and a table through a doorway to the right. Stairs near the door led to the second floor.

"I don't see any stuffed animals," Joe said. "Not that I expected to. That would be like waving a red flag with the word *Poacher* on it." He called over his shoulder, "I'll take the upstairs."

While Joe took the stairs two at a time, Frank looked around the living room. Daphne had to own a lot of hiking and camping equipment. He didn't see any of it there, so he decided to check the kitchen. Stepping through the kitchen doorway, he spotted a mud room piled high with tents, tools, packs, and other equipment. Frank wasn't surprised to see a gun rack on the wall. In the outback, it made sense. The rack held two rifles, neither of which seemed to be custom made. The shells were larger than the one he had found near the night glider and not silver in color. No match.

Dropping to a crouch, he began sifting through nylon bags of various colors. "Tent—sleeping bags —hey, what's this?"

He'd uncovered a wooden box about two feet long and ten inches wide. When he flipped open the lid, he saw half a dozen knives of varying sizes, all sheathed. Lying on top of them was an empty sheath. Frank fingered it absently before he realized that there was something familiar about it.

"I don't believe it," he whispered.

He stared at the distinctive swirls tooled into the red leather. It was exactly the same as the design on the handle of the knife Joe had found at Comet Creek National Park!

Chapter

Eight

"JOE, DOWN HERE!" Frank called to his brother. "You're not going to believe what I found."

Frank heard pounding footsteps on the stairs, and a second later Joe raced into the kitchen. "Is it the rifle? The custom-made job?"

In response, Frank held out the red leather knife sheath. When Joe saw it, he stopped short and exclaimed, "So Daphne *did* drop the knife! I was right. She must be the poacher, Frank. Otherwise, why wouldn't she have said the knife was hers?"

"I don't know," Frank admitted. "Working as a guide for Outback Adventures gives Daphne the perfect cover. No one would suspect her of harming wildlife." He turned the sheath over in his hands as he spoke. "But we still need more solid evidence. Even though we found her knife near the night glider, it hadn't been used. We need to find a gun or something that proves Daphne is in cahoots with Dennis Moore."

"If he's paying her, maybe she has a stash of money hidden somewhere," Joe suggested. He raised an eyebrow and grinned at his brother. "We're not done searching yet."

The two brothers poked through the rest of Daphne's things, but they didn't find a custom-made rifle or anything to indicate that Daphne was poaching for anyone else. After another half hour, Frank was ready to give up. "Let's get out of here before Daphne comes back and finds us," he told Joe.

Joe reluctantly got to his feet and followed Frank to the front door. "She's up to no good. I can feel it," he said, reaching for the doorknob. "I say we keep a close eye on her from now on—"

He broke off as he swung open the front door. "George!"

George did a double take when she saw the Hardys. "What are you doing here? Where's Daphne?"

"She's, uh, not exactly here," Joe began.

George peeked past Joe and Frank into the empty living room. "You broke in," she accused. "How could you?"

"For your information," Joe snapped, "Daphne might be a poacher."

"You've got a lot of nerve accusing her, Joe Hardy," George shot back.

Before she could say anything more, Frank stepped between her and Joe. "Hey! Will you two please chill out?" He told George about finding the leather sheath.

"You're sure it's Daphne's?" George asked.

Joe nodded. "I'm sorry I blew up at you, George, but we have to consider her a suspect. You won't tell her you saw us here, will you?"

George hesitated, but finally she smiled at Joe and said, "I guess I flew off the handle, too. You're wrong about Daphne, but I won't say anything."

Frank let out the breath he'd been holding. "Thanks for keeping an open mind, George. What are you doing here, anyway?"

"I was hoping Daphne could help me check out Ian and Marian Royce," George answered. "You heard about the opal theft, right?"

Frank nodded. "Nancy told us about it. She said something about the Royces possibly trying to pin the theft on Nellie to keep her from organizing the Yungis against them."

"Right," George confirmed. "I want to search their office."

"And you want someone to distract them?" Joe guessed. When George nodded, he grinned at her. "Well, Frank and I could come along. We aren't doing anything at the moment, are we?"

Their trip out to Tracker Jordan's sheep station could wait a little longer, Frank decided. Besides, with Nancy and Mick gone, George could use their help. "Count us in."

* * *

"Let me get this straight." Harold Apfelbach turned in the passenger seat and smiled at Joe, Frank, and George. "Frank and I will distract the Royces while you and George search their office."

"That's the general plan," Joe said, stifling a sigh. Glancing in the rearview mirror, he saw George's worried expression. She obviously wasn't crazy about Harold being in on their investigation, but he hadn't given them much of a choice. Harold had practically glued himself to them when they'd stopped for lunch at the Flat Hill Lodge, where Harold was staying. He'd seemed lonely and made it obvious that he wanted to join them. In the end they hadn't had the heart to tell him to bug off, so George told him about the case. Now the guy thought he was Sherlock Holmes.

"The office is in the back," George said as they pulled up across the street from the low brick building. "Joe, you and I can probably get in through a window, as long as Frank and Harold keep Ian and Marian busy."

"Don't worry," Harold said, patting the camera that was hanging around his neck. "I'll say Frank and I are doing an article on opals and I want to get some photos in their showroom."

As soon as Frank and Harold disappeared through the front door, Joe followed George to the back of the building. He peeked through the window into the office. "This must be the place," he said. "The window's open, so I doubt they have an alarm on—if they even have an alarm."

Seconds later they were inside the office. "I take

it we're looking for anything to show that the Royces set up Nellie," Joe said.

George nodded. "Right. But we should be careful about disturbing evidence and leaving finger-prints," she added, blushing as she realized who she was instructing.

"No problem," Joe assured her with a wink. While George went over to a file cabinet next to the safe, Joe concentrated on searching the desk. There was a disorderly pile of papers on top, but Joe didn't see anything special among them. Inside the top drawer he found only pens, pads, and pamphlets about Royce Mining, so he carefully shut it and reached for the file drawer.

"Locked, eh?" he murmured when it didn't budge. After taking out his pocketknife, he gently probed the lock, careful to leave no marks. It took only a few seconds to get the drawer open, and he plucked out a file at random. " 'Spectra Gems,' " he read aloud. "Doesn't look like much—just some of Marian's records from before she came to the outback. She was a buyer for a gem business in Sydney, Spectra Gems. That must be how she got the experience to run the mine here."

He was about to close the file, when a series of clipped articles caught his eye. "Wait a second. Check out this headline. 'Gem Exec Implicated in Scandal,' " he read. "It's about Marian."

"You're kidding." George was next to him in an instant, skimming the article. "Wow, read this! Two years ago she was suspected of stealing money from Spectra Gems. She wasn't convicted, but it looks like the scandal pretty much wrecked her career in Sydney."

"So maybe Marian Royce isn't above breaking the law," Joe added.

George tapped the file, thinking. "It's starting to make sense—why she'd move way out here when she obviously hates the outback. She probably wanted to make a new start where people wouldn't know what had happened."

"We still haven't found any proof that she and Ian are setting up Nellie, though," Joe reminded her.

George bent over the desk's file drawer. "Let's keep looking," she said. "Tax files, bank statements . . ." She drew in her breath as she pulled out a file from the back of the drawer. "Mabo!" she announced triumphantly. "There's a whole file on Nellie!"

Joe peered over George's shoulder while she opened the file. In it were letters from Nellie stating the Yungis' objection to their mining sacred land. More recent correspondence was from a lawyer in Brisbane who was representing the Yungis.

"Look at this one," George said. It was a letter from the lawyer, dated just a week earlier. In it, he informed the Royces of the Yungis' petition to have ownership of the mine revert to the tribe. "Look what someone wrote in the margins."

Joe caught the words *Outrageous!* and *No deal.* George was pointing to a note at the bottom of the page—"Stop Mabo at all costs."

"At all costs, huh," Joe said. "I wonder if that includes setting Nellie up."

George opened her mouth to answer, then turned her head sharply toward the door. "Joe, footsteps!"

A second later Frank's voice came from right outside the door. "Mrs. Royce, I really don't want you to go to any trouble. Harold and I can pick up the brochures about the opals and the mine another time."

"It's no trouble at all," Marian's answer came through the door. "They're right here in the office."

Joe quickly shoved the files back into the drawer. The doorknob rattled, causing both him and George to jump. Joe looked around wildly, but he didn't see where they could hide.

In a second Marian Royce was going to catch them going through her office!

Chapter

Nine

FRANK GRABBED Marian's arm to stop her from opening the office door. "Harold and I really have to go," he said urgently. "Why don't we schedule an appointment for tomorrow and—"

"What could possibly be so urgent out here?" Marian asked, raising a dubious eyebrow at him.

"I want to get a photograph of you in the showroom before the light changes," Harold put in.

Marian simply waved away their objections. Before Frank could say anything more, she pushed open the office door and stepped inside. Frank held his breath and followed, with Harold right behind him.

"The office is still a little messy," Marian said, stepping gingerly around some broken glass. "We had a robbery early this morning. All the black opals we had were stolen. They're worth a small fortune."

Frank barely listened while Harold told Marian how sorry he was. Frank checked around quickly for Joe and George.

"I have some brochures in the desk." Marian said. Frank had just caught sight of one of George's sneaker tips sticking out from under the desk. "Wait!" he called.

Marian turned and stared at him. "Yes?"

Frank searched his mind for something, anything, to say to keep her away from that desk. "To tell you the truth, I'm much more interested in hearing about the robbery. Do you know who did it?"

"Nellie Mabo, a troublemaker from the Yungi settlement," Marian said without hesitation. "The police haven't caught her yet, but her scarf was found right next to the safe."

Marian was obviously ready to convict Nellie, even before the police had finished investigating, Frank thought. He decided to see if he could get Marian to reveal anything to back up Nancy and George's theory that the Royces had set up Nellie. Keeping his tone casual, he said, "Didn't I hear something about a conflict between you and the Yungis? Something about your mine being on sacred Aboriginal land?"

"What does that have to do with the stolen opals?" Harold asked blankly.

"That's my question exactly," Marian added. She stared suspiciously at Frank. "My husband and

I are the victims here, not Nellie Mabo and the Yungis."

"Yes, of course," Frank said quickly.

Marian's eyes flashed with anger. "We've worked hard to make a success of the mine from the day we bought the land from Paul Kidder."

Frank's ears perked up at the mention of Paul Kidder. George had mentioned him when she'd filled in Joe and him on the opal theft. Paul was the cook at the Flat Hill Lodge's diner, Frank remembered. From what George had said, he felt cheated by the Royces and was so bitter that the two girls considered him a suspect in the theft, too.

"Paul Kidder must have regretted selling the mine, huh?" Frank said to Marian.

"That's putting it mildly," she answered. "Ever since we found opals in the mine, Paul has been telling everyone about how Ian and I cheated him."

"Well, um, did you?" Harold asked.

"Certainly not!" Marian replied defensively. "It's not our fault that he sank his mining shafts in the wrong places. He was grateful to us for taking the mine off his hands. Now he acts as if we stole it from him."

As far as Frank was concerned, that sounded like a pretty solid motive for theft. "Maybe Kidder decided to get back at you by helping himself to some of the profits," he commented.

Marian gave him a sideways look. "Are you saying that he might have stolen the black opals?" When Frank merely shrugged, she shook her head firmly. "No, no, no. Nellie Mabo is the thief. I know it, and the police know it. Before he left, the police officer told us that so far she's the top suspect."

"Mmm" was all Frank said. Before Marian could continue toward the desk, he said to Harold, "Didn't you want to buy some opals out in the showroom?"

Harold looked at him blankly, then blinked. "Oh—yes. I really do want to do that now."

This time Marian didn't object. Frank breathed a sigh of relief when she led the way back to the showroom and closed the office door behind her. Although there were no black opals, the glass case held numerous lighter, less expensive stones that were flecked with fiery sparks of color. Harold bought three stones, and then he and Frank left. They were climbing into the Range Rover when Joe and George appeared around the corner of the building. As the two of them jumped into the backseat, Joe said, "Let's go."

As Frank started the engine, he turned to George and said, "You might be right about the Royces setting up Nellie. You heard how touchy Marian got when I brought up the Yungis' claim to the sacred land."

"We didn't find any proof that they're setting her up," George said, "but it looks as if Marian might not be the most ethical person in the world."

"What about that Kidder guy?" Joe asked. "He definitely has a motive for stealing the opals."

George nodded her agreement. "I'm going to check him out next." She sighed and leaned back against the seat. "I feel as if it could take forever to get to the bottom of this," she said. "I hope Nancy and Mick are having better luck on their end."

"Sorry for the delay," Gil said to Nancy and Mick on Tuesday morning.

"That's okay," Nancy said. Gil had had to cut their flight short the afternoon before when his plane's fuel line became clogged again. The town where they'd landed had been so small that Nancy wasn't sure it even had a name, but a store owner put them up while Gil fixed the line. It had taken him until that morning to get the plane in good enough shape to fly to the coast, where they now were in a rental car.

"We appreciate your making this detour to Airlie Beach," Mick added. "And for waiting while we booked rooms at the youth hostel." Gil's clients were in a town called Mackay, to the south. But he'd insisted on flying directly to Airlie Beach so Nancy and Mick could look for Nellie right away.

"Are you sure you don't mind taking us to the harbor?" Nancy asked.

"It's no problem," Gil assured her. "As long as I'm here, I can take care of some business. My clients already know I'm going to be late, and Shute Harbour is right on my way."

"That's where all the boats to the Whitsunday Islands leave from," Mick explained. "If Nellie is on the run, maybe she's planning to hide out on one of the islands. Some of them are quite remote."

As they drove down the coastal road, a sea breeze

whipped through Nancy's hair. She could see brilliant turquoise water stretching out from the shoreline to her right and the forested peaks of half a dozen islands dotting the horizon. "No wonder so many people come here," she said. "It's gorgeous."

"You haven't even seen the coral reefs yet," Mick said. He smiled, but Nancy could tell that his mind was on finding Nellie, not on the scenery.

Before long Nancy caught sight of a port with dozens of ships moored along its piers. The place was bustling with cars, buses, and people heading to and from the boats. "Shute Harbour?" she guessed.

Gil nodded. "Looks busy. If you like, I can help you two look around before I take care of my business. I guess my clients can wait a few minutes longer."

"Thanks, Gil," Mick said. "I appreciate it."

After finding a spot in the crowded parking lot, the three of them hurried to the dock area. "Let's start by asking if anyone's seen Nellie," Mick suggested. He opened his wallet and pulled out a snapshot of him and Nellie. "We can show this around."

"I'll check the ticket offices," Nancy offered. She pointed at the warehouses and shipping offices lining the harbor. "We can show her picture at those places, too. If we split up, we could work more efficiently. Do you have any other photos of Nellie?"

"This is the only one," Mick answered. He tapped the photo as his eyes roved over the docks.

"I guess we'll just have to—" Mick froze, his eyes fixed on something behind Nancy.

"Mick? What is it?" As soon as she turned around, Nancy saw what had gotten his attention. "Nellie!" she said. The girl had just come out of an office, a wary expression on her face. Nancy thought she spotted a bandage on Nellie's forearm.

Gil snapped his head around. "This is too good to be true," he said under his breath.

"Nellie! Am I glad to see you!" Mick waved his hands and started toward her. When Nellie saw him, she did a double take. Even from across the dock, Nancy saw the dread on the young woman's face.

"Nellie, we want to help," Nancy called out.

Nellie didn't appear to have heard her. In fact, she was backing away from them, more terrified every second.

"What's going on? Why is she acting like that?" Mick said under his breath. "Nellie, wait!"

Without a word, Nellie turned and fled.

Chapter

Ten

NANCY, QUICK! We can't lose her," Mick cried, sprinting after Nellie.

Nancy had already started running. "I'm right behind you," she yelled. She could hear Gil behind her, but she kept her gaze focused on the yellow scarf Nellie wore in her hair. Nellie raced across the street and behind a row of buses at the edge of the dock. Mick was about thirty feet behind her. He shot behind the buses, too, but Nancy decided to circle around in front of them, where people were waiting beneath cement canopies.

"Oh!" Nancy yelled, as she rammed into two guys with backpacks. "Are you all right—"

Suddenly a flash of yellow at the front of the bus caught her eye. "Nellie!" She was only about ten feet away. When she spotted Nancy, Nellie headed for the dock.

"Mick, this way!" Nancy yelled. She glanced over her shoulder just long enough to spot Mick and Gil emerge from between the buses. Then she took off after Nellie again. The dock was a maze of piers and people and luggage. "Hey," one man yelled as Nellie pushed past him, scattering his luggage. A swarm of people was just debarking from one of the boats, and Nancy kept losing sight of Nellie's yellow scarf in the crowd.

"Excuse us," Mick yelled. Nancy could hear the frustration in his voice as he skirted one group. "Where *is* she?" he muttered frantically.

Gil had taken off to the right. Suddenly he yelled and pointed toward a metal forklift that was off-loading wooden crates from one of the ships. Nellie ducked behind the crates as Nancy, Mick, and Gil all zeroed in on the forklift at the same time.

"Nellie, please stop!" Mick called out. "We just want to talk to—"

At that moment a wall of crates started falling toward them. Nancy, Mick, and Gil all jumped back as the crates clattered to the ground. Nancy tried to keep her eyes on Nellie, but the pile of crates blocked her view. When she finally managed to get around them, she didn't see Nellie anywhere. As Mick and Gil joined her, she cried, "We've lost her!"

Mick frowned darkly. "I don't know how we're going to—"

The rest of what he said was drowned out by a loud whistle from a boat that was just pulling away from the dock. Tourists were leaning against the railing, laughing and waving. Nancy was about to turn her attention back to the dock, when a sudden movement on the ship's deck caught her attention.

"Mick!" Nancy grabbed his arm and pointed. "Up there. Isn't that Nellie?" The ship was fifty feet away, but Nancy was fairly sure that she recognized the figure disappearing through a doorway on the ship.

"Nellie!" Mick shouted, confirming her guess. "I can't believe this. We're too late."

The boat, the *Island Princess,* was already twenty yards out. The entrance from the dock was now cordoned off, and a man was just putting a pile of ticket stubs into a metal strongbox.

"Come on," Nancy said to Mick and Gil. "Let's talk to him."

"Can you tell us where the *Island Princess* is headed?" Mick asked when they got to the man.

The man barely looked up from the clipboard he was writing on. "Long Island, Hamilton Island, Lindeman Island, Shaw Island, Thomas Island." He rattled off the list so quickly that Nancy could barely remember all the names.

"We can't search every single one of those places," Mick said, frowning.

"Do you remember seeing an Aborigine girl get on the boat?" Nancy asked the man. "She was wearing a yellow scarf."

"Look, mate, I can't keep track of every . . ." His voice trailed off, and he rubbed his chin. "Yellow scarf, you say?"

"Yes," Gil said. "Do you know where she was going?"

"I do," the man said, nodding "Heading for Thomas Island, she was. I only remember because she almost missed the boat. She was the last one on."

Mick squeezed Nancy's hand excitedly. "Great! When does the next boat leave?"

"Same time tomorrow," the man replied. "The ticket office is over—"

"Tomorrow?" Mick cut in. "Isn't there any other boat going to Thomas Island today?"

"Sorry," the man said, shaking his head.

Nancy exchanged a frustrated look with Mick. "Thanks anyway," she told the man. Then she, Mick, and Gil stepped away.

"Tough break," Gil said, clapping Mick on the shoulder. "I hate to desert you, but my clients are waiting."

"Don't worry about it," Mick told him. "You've already done a lot to help us. Thanks, Gil." As Gil walked back toward the parking lot, Mick stared out over Shute Harbour. "What just happened?" he asked. "Why would Nellie run from us like that?"

Nancy didn't have an answer. "I just wish there was some way we could follow her." She pointed to a smaller wooden pier next to the commercial docks. Dozens of sailboats and power boats were moored there. "Those look like private boats, don't they?"

"Yeah," Mick said, shrugging. "So?"

"So, do you think someone would be willing to hire out his boat to a couple of tourists who want to visit the Great Barrier Reef?"

A slow smile spread over Mick's face. "Out by Thomas Island, for instance? Sure. Why not? Maybe there's a way to catch up with Nellie after all."

"The man at Shute Harbour wasn't kidding when he told us that Thomas Island is deserted," Nancy said. "We haven't seen anyone so far except for those three people waiting for the boat."

"I'm just glad we made it here before the *Island Princess*," Mick added.

They were sitting at one end of a curved beach, next to the island's only dock, waiting for the passenger boat to arrive. There was a small national parks information hut near the docks, and a camping area at the other end of the beach, several hundred yards away. Otherwise, the island was completely unspoiled. Behind them, forested hills rose up dramatically. A soft wind rustled through the wide fronds of the pandanus palms clustered at the edge of the sand.

"I think I see it," Mick said, breaking into Nancy's thoughts.

Following his gaze, Nancy could make out the shape of the approaching ship. "We'd better get out of sight."

By the time the ship docked, Nancy and Mick were crouched behind a cluster of palms just off the beach. Only one passenger got off the boat. When Nancy saw the woman's dark skin and the yellow scarf in her hair, she let out a sigh of relief. "It's Nellie."

"This time, I'm not letting her out of my sight," Mick whispered. "Let's follow her."

"Not too close," Nancy cautioned. "She'll just run away again."

Looking ahead, she saw that Nellie had stopped at the national parks hut. A dark-skinned man in a khaki uniform came to the doorway and gave Nellie a warm smile, clapping her around the shoulder. The two spoke for several minutes, then Nellie set off into the forested hills.

"Do you recognize that man?" Nancy whispered to Mick as the ranger disappeared into the hut again. "Nellie seems to know him."

"I've never seen—" Mick started to shake his head, then caught himself. "Wait! Nellie did say something to me once about a friend of hers who's a national parks ranger. I'm pretty sure she said he worked in the Whitsundays."

Nancy frowned. "If she's planning to hide out here, she might have warned him to keep anyone off her trail. Let's hope he doesn't notice us."

She and Mick quietly skirted the hut, then started down the path Nellie had taken. They moved as quietly as they could. Nancy could just see Nellie's yellow scarf through the trees ahead.

Thomas Island was thickly wooded, and Nancy

and Mick had good cover as they followed Nellie. They caught sight of the water only once, when the path came out above a small cove where a boat was moored.

They had been hiking for over an hour, when Mick stopped on the path in front of Nancy. He held a finger to his lips, then pointed. A few hundred feet ahead, the dense forest opened into a small clearing. Nellie had stopped there and was sitting on a rock. Nancy couldn't see her clearly, but it looked as if she was eating. Just then Nancy's stomach started growling. Mick smiled at her, then whispered. "We might as well eat, too."

They sat at the edge of the path, and Mick pulled out two sandwiches they had bought earlier that day.

Nancy was just biting into her sandwich when a rustling to the left of the path caught her attention. She stared into the brush but couldn't see what had made the noise.

"Probably just an animal," Mick whispered.

Glancing ahead to the clearing, Nancy saw that Nellie was still sitting there, eating. She didn't appear to have heard them or the rustling noise. "Let's try to get a quick look at it," Nancy whispered, getting to her feet. "Seeing the wildlife around here is a once-in-a-lifetime chance."

Slowly she and Mick tiptoed into the woods. She paused when she heard the noise again. It seemed to be coming from behind a thick bush with fragrant red flowers on it. Quietly Nancy inched her way around the bush.

"Nothing," she whispered, letting out a sigh as she looked around. "Whatever it was, it's gone now."

"Well, I doubt we've seen the last of the wild things here," Mick told her. "Just about every inch of Australia is crawling with unusual creatures."

"Plants, too," Nancy said. "I've never seen flowers quite like those red ones." She pointed to the bushy shrub. "They smell like perfume, but, I don't know, they're kind of harsh smelling at the same time." Shaking herself, Nancy started back to the path. The last thing they needed to do was lose Nellie.

When they got back to their packs, Nancy was relieved to see that Nellie was still sitting in the clearing ahead. "I need something to drink," Nancy whispered, and unzipped the lower compartment to reach for her water bottle. Instead her hand touched something else.

"Ugh!" Nancy jerked her hand back and saw the glistening scales of a brown snake that was now thrashing wildly.

"What's the matter, Nancy?" Mick bent over the pack and saw the snake. "That's a taipan," he said, his face going completely white. "It's the deadliest snake in Australia!"

Everything Nancy had ever read about poisonous snakes said that they usually didn't attack—unless provoked. And this one didn't seem at all happy about being disturbed. Nancy backed away slowly from her pack, trying to hold back the wave of fear that rose inside her. Keeping her voice to a whisper, she said, "Let's just try to—"

She broke off with a gasp as the taipan's head darted through the opening and shot toward Mick's leg.

"No!" Nancy cried.

It was too late. All she could do was watch in horror as the deadly snake sank its fangs into Mick's jeans. In seconds the taipan struck once, twice, three times.

Then it slithered off into the woods.

Chapter

Eleven

MICK STUMBLED, dazed. "What?"

"Careful!" Nancy jumped to support him. "Sit down and don't move. The poison will only spread faster." Once Mick was seated, she reached frantically for her pack. "The snakebite kit's in here somewhere." She knew it could be just a matter of seconds before . . .

A sensation of dread welled up from the pit of Nancy's stomach, spreading to every inch of her body. "You have to pull through, Mick. You mean too much to me!" She frantically groped for the snakebite kit.

"Here it is," she cried, pulling out the kit. "Okay, show me where—"

"Nancy, calm down! I think I'm okay."

It took a second for his words to sink in. "What?" She sat back on her heels and stared at him. Mick had pushed up the cuff of his jeans and was pointing at his ankle. "The bites didn't go through to my skin," he said. "I'm okay."

Looking closely, Nancy realized that he was right. The skin on his ankle was smooth—there were no bite marks. "But how?"

"Taipans are deadly, but their fangs aren't very long. I guess my jeans were thick enough to keep the fangs from breaking through to my skin."

"Thank goodness!" Nancy said. She felt so weak that she actually had to sit down. Glancing at Mick, she saw that he was watching her, a smile on his face.

"Nancy, did you mean what you said about—"

Nancy jolted upright. "Nellie! I totally forgot about her." She whipped her head around to look at the clearing.

It was deserted.

"We've lost her. I don't believe this," Mick said, shaking his head. He moved to pick up his pack, but Nancy stopped him.

"She's long gone by now," she said. "With the commotion we just made, she must have heard us. She'll make sure we don't find her now. . . ." Nancy's voice trailed off as she had a sudden thought.

"Mick, that taipan didn't zip itself into my pack. Someone put it there."

"You think Nellie did it?" Mick asked after a

long pause. "Running away from us is one thing, but trying to kill us?" He shook his head adamantly. "You're wrong. Nellie wouldn't do it, that's all."

"It wouldn't have been possible for her to sneak back here from that clearing and get away again without our noticing. We were only gone for a minute or two," Nancy said, thinking out loud. "But if she didn't put the taipan in my pack, who did?"

Mick frowned and crossed his arms over his chest. "That noise we heard in the forest—maybe it was someone else. While we were checking it out, the person could have put the snake in your pack." He let out his breath in a rush, then raised an eyebrow at Nancy. "Maybe the guy we saw Nellie talking to?"

"He's the only person I can think of who could have followed us," Nancy agreed. "Let's see what we can find out from him."

After double-checking their packs for more snakes, she and Mick hiked back to the wooden hut near the dock. As they approached, the young man appeared in the doorway.

"Afternoon," Mick began, smiling at him. "Had many hikers on this trail today?" he asked, pointing up the trail they'd taken.

"One or two," the ranger said. He crossed his arms over his chest and waited.

"Being a ranger must be intense," Nancy said, flashing him an impressed smile. "What with maintaining the trails and helping out all the hikers. Have you been out on any of the trails today?"

"Can't say I have."

He wasn't exactly bubbling over with information, Nancy thought. She decided to try a more blunt approach. "The reason we're asking is because someone put a taipan in my pack," she told him. "We could have been killed."

"What?" The ranger blinked in surprise, then muttered under his breath, "It must be a coincidence."

"What are you talking about?" Mick asked.

"Someone at the campsite captured a taipan yesterday—put it in a large plastic water container," the ranger said.

"Someone took the container?" Nancy guessed.

The man hesitated, then said, "He noticed it was missing when he packed up to leave today. As I said, it's probably a coincidence." He became guarded again. "I cannot keep track of every person who sets foot on this island. There are hundreds of coves where private boats could dock. Now, if you'll excuse me, I have work to do."

With that, the ranger went back inside the hut. "What's with him?" Mick whispered to Nancy.

She shrugged. "I don't know whether to believe him or not, and there's no one around we can ask to find out whether he left the parks hut." While they walked toward the dock, she started thinking ahead to what their next step should be. "We can forget about finding Nellie. There are too many places she could hide—we could never search them all. I say we go back to Shute Harbour and talk to people in the building we saw her come out of. We might get a better idea of what's really going on and why she won't talk to us."

"I hate to leave here," Mick said, gazing at the green hills behind them, "but I guess you're right."

After checking her watch, Nancy added, "It's already three o'clock. We probably won't make it back to the harbor before the office closes. But"—she nodded toward their boat, which was tied to one of the dock's mooring posts—"the boat we rented does have snorkeling equipment. . . ."

"I don't think I ever spent so much time on the phone as we did this morning," Joe grumbled Tuesday afternoon. He leaned back in the passenger seat and let the hot wind whip over his face and arms. "It feels great to finally get outside."

"At least Dad was able to give us some info on Dennis Moore. I can't believe it—the guy's been implicated in half a dozen major international poaching operations! Elephants and rhinos out of Kenya, the white Arctic fox . . ." Frank let out a whistle. "What a sleazeball."

"A smart sleazeball. He's never gone to jail," Joe pointed out. Reaching into his pocket, he pulled out the folded photograph of Dennis Moore that their father had faxed to them at Outback Adventures. He unfolded the sheet and stared at the man's angular face, slicked-back dark hair, and widely set eyes. "'Forty-six years old, six feet tall, gray eyes, medium build,'" Joe read from the typed description at the bottom of the photo.

He and Frank had called their father that morning, but it had taken Fenton Hardy several hours to get information on Dennis Moore from his contacts. Now Frank and Joe were driving to the Flat Hill Lodge to see if they could come up with any proof linking Moore to the shootings of the rare animals at Comet Creek.

"Let's hope Moore is back from the aboriginal communities by now," Frank said as he turned onto the main street. "We should be careful, though. If he is behind the poaching, chances are he knows we're investigating him. Whoever pushed you off the ledge probably told Moore that we're going after the poacher."

A few moments later he pulled to a stop in front of the Flat Hill Lodge. As they hopped out, Joe saw Daphne coming out of the Outback Adventures office. He did a double take when he saw the tall man who stepped out after her.

"Frank," Joe called softly. Frank was heading toward the lodge. "Am I hallucinating, or is that Dennis Moore?"

Frank turned and glanced across the street, then looked at the faxed picture Joe held out. "You're right!" he exclaimed under his breath. "What's he doing with Daphne?"

Joe shrugged, keeping his eyes on Moore and Daphne. The two spoke briefly, then Daphne got into her Range Rover and drove away, heading east. Moore crossed the street toward the lodge. When he saw Frank and Joe, the man's gaze narrowed briefly.

"Hi. How's it going?" Joe asked casually. He

wasn't sure what he hoped to accomplish, but he couldn't pass up an opportunity to talk to Dennis Moore. "Are you going bush walking with Outback Adventures?"

Moore stopped a few feet from Frank and Joe and gave them a look Joe couldn't quite read. "Might be," he answered. "What's it to you two?"

"We're friends of Gil Strickland and Daphne Whooten," Frank said. He introduced himself and Joe, then said, "You won't find a better guide than Daphne, especially if you want to see the wildlife."

The corners of Dennis Moore's mouth twisted up in the slightest smile. "Miss Whooten seems like a right intelligent girl. If I was going bush walking, I wouldn't hesitate to take her as a guide."

"The Comet Creek gorges are pretty amazing," Joe said. "You should really see them, if you're on vacation here."

"I'm here on business, actually," Moore said smoothly. "Import-export. I've been out at the Yungis' community making a deal to buy their bark carvings. There's a market for them in tourist centers along the coast and abroad. I'm returning to Melbourne today, though." Moore nodded, then continued toward the lodge. "G'day."

"Hmm." Joe kept his eyes on Dennis Moore until he disappeared inside the lodge. Then he turned to Frank. "Didn't that explanation seem a little rehearsed to you? And he was definitely evasive about what he was doing talking to Daphne. I mean, why would an importer go to Gil's office?"

"But if Moore had hired Daphne to poach for him, would he really be dumb enough to be seen with her in a public place? It doesn't make sense," Frank said.

Joe took a deep breath and let it out slowly. "No, but why else would he—"

"G'day." Harold's voice spoke up right behind Joe. "What are you two up to?"

Frank turned to see the photographer standing on the sidewalk, his aluminum camera case hanging from his shoulder. "Uh, Joe and I were just, uh—" Actually, he wasn't sure what they were going to do, but he knew they didn't need an amateur around.

"I was thinking of going walkabout outside of Flat Hill to get some photos, but if you two are doing something else . . ." Harold looked expectantly at them.

"Don't drop everything for us," Joe said quickly. "We're really not up to anything special. Nothing as exciting as photographing the outback."

Harold nodded eagerly. "I found a goanna's nest earlier. If I'm lucky, I'll be able to capture the precise moment its eggs hatch. Why don't you come with me? It should be amazing."

"Sounds fascinating," Joe said halfheartedly.

Frank knew he and Joe couldn't afford to waste the rest of the day. Why did Harold have to choose them to be his best buddies?

Frank blinked as an idea came to him. Suddenly he knew exactly what to do. Joe wasn't going to like it, but . . . "Why don't you and Joe go?" Frank suggested, smiling brightly at Harold.

"What!" Joe shot him a surprised look.

"I wish I could come along," Frank said quickly, "but I, uh, promised Gil I'd water his plants."

Harold didn't seem to notice how lame his excuse was. "Hey, that'd be great. Let's go, Joe."

Frank ignored the glare Joe was shooting his way. "So it's settled. Well, I guess I'd better get going. See you back at Gil's, Joe." Before Joe could say anything more, Frank got into their Range Rover and pulled away with a wave.

As he drove down the street, he wondered aloud, "Now what?" He and Joe had already spoken to Dennis Moore, but they hadn't been to Tracker Jordan's sheep station yet. Gil had said the station was to the west, on the opposite side of Flat Hill from the national park. The trip was an hour and a half each way—if he was fast, he could make it there and back before dark. Frank didn't think he'd have any problem finding the station. There was probably only one road going west.

Just then he saw Daphne's white Rover passing him. She was driving it, and George was now in the passenger seat. Hitting the gas, Frank sped up and pulled even with them.

"How's it going?" he called loudly.

Daphne just gave him a cool once-over and started to speed up, but George said something to her. A moment later Daphne slowed to a stop. When Frank pulled up next to her, Daphne nodded toward the empty passenger seat and asked, "Where's your sidekick, the outdoor wonder boy?"

Frank wasn't crazy about her sarcastic tone, but decided not to make the situation any worse. "Joe's photographing goannas and dust balls with Harold Apfelbach," he answered with a shrug. "What are you two up to?"

"Daphne told me that Paul Kidder lives in a caravan park west of town," George said. "We're going to check it out. He should be cooking at the lodge now, so it'll be safe."

"Oh, yeah?" Frank gazed at some ropes sticking out from beneath a tarp in the rear of Daphne's Rover. If Daphne and George were going to be inside Kidder's caravan, he might be able to search Daphne's vehicle. Maybe he could find out what Dennis Moore had been talking to Daphne about, too. "Why don't I go with you? I could keep watch while you two search his place," he offered.

"Suit yourself," Daphne said, shrugging. Then she hit the gas and roared off.

The road wound through a thicket of straggly trees before stretching out into the flat, open outback. Half a dozen caravans were parked beneath the trees. Frank followed the girls to a run-down caravan that was set up on cinder blocks. It was white, with a cracked brown stripe around the side. The curtains fluttering in the open windows were so old and faded that he couldn't even tell what color they were supposed to be. A woman and three children were outside one of the other caravans, but they paid no attention to Daphne, George, and Frank.

"Here goes nothing," George said, knocking on the caravan door. When there was no answer, she and Daphne went inside.

As soon as they were out of sight, Frank sauntered over to the back of Daphne's Range Rover. He glanced briefly at the caravan windows, then lifted the tarp and peered underneath it. A quick search turned up some ropes, a first-aid kit, a tent, and a few tools. Frank stepped around to the front of the Rover but didn't see a rifle there, either. He leaned against the back fender and let out a sigh. If Daphne was the poacher, she wasn't keeping the custom-made rifle at home or in her car.

Frank looked up at the sound of a truck approaching. He wasn't sure what kind of vehicle Paul Kidder drove, but he didn't think George and Daphne wanted to risk getting caught.

"Someone's driving this way," he called, jogging over to one of the caravan's windows and pushing aside the curtains. "A truck—I think it's black."

"We're almost done." George closed the two wooden drawers beneath a messy bunk, then quickly turned to the jumble of assorted junk on a shelf at the bunk's head.

"So far, it doesn't look like Paul Kidder is the man you're looking for," Daphne said from the kitchen area.

Frank shifted from foot to foot. "I don't want to rush you two, but that truck is getting closer."

Suddenly George stood bolt upright. "Wow!" she

exclaimed, staring into an old cigar box she had just opened. "Look at this!"

She reached into the box, pulled out a dark object, and held it up. Even from outside the caravan, Frank saw the fiery sparkle of the stone.

"Is this what I think it is?" George asked Daphne.

Daphne's gray eyes widened. "Looks to me like you've found yourself a black opal."

Chapter

Twelve

For a moment they all just stared at the opal. Frank was amazed by the thousands of flecks of red, orange, and purple that sparkled in the dark stone.

Daphne broke the silence. "That's about half an inch around. Must be worth a bundle."

George nodded excitedly. "Now we just have to find the rest of—" She broke off, staring out the window in dismay. "That truck—it's driving right up here." She dropped the cigar box on Kidder's bunk, then hurried toward the door.

Frank had been so caught up staring at the opal that he'd forgotten about the truck. It was now pulling to a stop beneath the trees. Through the dusty windshield, Frank saw a grizzled-looking man in his sixties. The man got out of his truck and walked toward the caravan.

"G'day," he greeted Frank with a slow nod. "'Aven't I seen you at the lodge?" Before Frank could answer, the man spotted George in the caravan's doorway. "Hey! What's going on?" he demanded.

"That's exactly what we'd like to know, Mr. Kidder," George said. She stepped down to the ground and strode over to him, holding out the black opal. "What are you doing with this?"

Paul Kidder snatched the opal from George, his pale eyes flashing with anger. "I don't know who you are, but you've got no right to go through my things. I ought to call the police!" His eyes widened when he saw Daphne stepping out of the caravan. "Daphne Whooten? When did you take up with hoodlums?"

"Paul, these people are looking for the person who stole a bag of black opals from Ian and Marian," Daphne explained. "I'm beginning to think they've found their man."

"I bet the rest of the opals are here somewhere," George added angrily.

Paul Kidder stared at them blankly, then rubbed his stubble of beard. "You think I stole those opals?" he finally asked. Frank thought he seemed genuinely confused by the accusation.

"Um, Mr. Kidder, if you didn't steal the opals, then what are you doing with that?" Frank asked, nodding toward the stone the older man clutched in his wrinkled hand.

"This?" A faraway look came into Paul Kidder's eyes as he rubbed the stone between his callused fingers. "It's the first opal I ever found as a miner. Forty-seven years ago, I dug it up right where Royce Mining is now. Kept it for luck."

George looked skeptically at the miner. "It looks pretty valuable. Why wouldn't you sell it?"

"Miners can be very superstitious," Daphne put in. "Keeping your first opal is a common practice."

"Not that it's done me any good," Kidder added bitterly. "After finding this beaut, I dug up nothing but third-rate potch. Then Ian and Marian move in and strike it rich on my site."

Giving the older man a probing look, George said, "I guess you must have been pretty upset."

"I know what you're trying to insinuate," Kidder said angrily. "I never stole anything from anyone. I'm tuckered enough, working two shifts at the lodge. Just came back for a rest before the dinner rush. I don't need to take this from you know-it-alls. Now, get out of here, before I call the police." Kidder stormed inside his trailer and slammed the door.

Frank, George, and Daphne waited until they were at their cars before saying anything. "He hardly looks as if he's come into a large amount of money recently," Daphne said in a low voice, glancing back at Kidder's run-down caravan and truck.

"He could be planning to move somewhere else and make a fresh start with the money from the stolen opals," George said. "But my gut feeling is that he's just a poor miner who kept his first opal for good luck, as he said."

Frank had to agree. "I wouldn't rule him out completely, but if I were you I'd concentrate more on the theory that the Royces are setting up Nellie."

George nodded, then looked expectantly at Frank and Daphne. "What do we do now?"

"Paperwork. I've got piles of it waiting for me at the Outback Adventures office," Daphne answered, sliding in behind the wheel.

"It must be hard to keep up, what with clients stopping by the Outback Adventures office," Frank said. "Didn't I see someone at the office today?"

"If you want to know about Dennis Moore, why don't you ask me straight out?" Daphne responded angrily. "Is this an interrogation, or am I free to go?"

"I was wondering what he wanted, that's all," Frank said. "Moore has been implicated in poaching in the past, you know." He couldn't help wondering why she was so touchy—unless she had something to hide.

"We didn't talk about anything that concerns you," Daphne said curtly. "Are you coming with me?" she asked George.

"If you're busy, I can hitch a ride back with Frank," George said.

Frank checked his watch and realized that he'd spent longer there than he'd anticipated. It was already late afternoon—the sun was getting lower in the sky. Frank doubted there was enough time to go to Tracker Jordan's station and back before dark. He and Joe would have to wait until the morning. Turning to George, Frank said, "Hop in. Joe and Harold will probably be back from photographing soon. Maybe we can all get something to eat."

"See you," Daphne said. She gave George a smile but ignored Frank. With a quick wave, she drove off.

"What was that about?" George asked Frank as he turned the key in the ignition. She didn't say anything when Frank told her about seeing Daphne and Dennis Moore. Frank could tell it was hard for her to remain neutral, when she and Daphne were becoming friends, but he wasn't sure what he could do to make the situation easier.

When they got back to Flat Hill, Frank spotted Harold and Joe walking toward the lodge. "Get any good shots?" Frank called out, pulling up next to them.

"The goanna eggs were gone. I think a snake got them. We got great shots of red kangaroos and some emu just outside town, though," Harold answered.

While Harold described their walk, Joe came over to the driver's door and whispered to Frank, "Where did you go?"

"I was going to Jordan's station, but I got held up," Frank said, without going into any details. "I didn't want to get stuck out there after dark, so we'll go tomorrow morning instead."

Apparently Harold heard him. "Imagine being

stuck in the outback at night," he said, grimacing. "No photograph would be worth it."

"I don't know," Joe said. "We just saw Daphne heading out toward the national park. If she can do it, so can we—"

"You saw Daphne driving *out* of town?" Frank cut in. "She just told George and me she had to do paperwork at the Outback Adventures office."

Joe stared at Frank, frowning. "Maybe she's going on a little mission for Dennis Moore."

"Why do you guys have to be suspicious of everything Daphne does?" George objected. "She could have a perfectly good reason."

"Yeah, right," Joe scoffed. "I think we should follow her, Frank."

"Count me out," George said, getting out of the Range Rover. Frank could tell she wasn't happy, but he had to agree with Joe.

"Let's go," Harold said. Before Frank could object, he climbed into the backseat.

Joe kept his eyes focused on the cloud of dust in the distance. Daphne's Range Rover had come into view as soon as they'd gotten clear of the town. She was a good half mile ahead of them, but they were gaining.

Joe noticed another vehicle driving across the outback from the west, kicking up a dusty trail as it headed toward the road they were on. Joe opened the glove compartment and pulled out the binoculars he had borrowed from Gil. "Who have we here?" he wondered aloud, focusing on the vehicle, which had stopped next to Daphne's car. "Red pickup, a guy with a beard . . ."

"Tracker Jordan?" Frank guessed.

Joe lowered the binoculars. "Bingo. He and Daphne are having some kind of rendezvous."

Frank pulled off the road and drove closer to the gum trees that dotted the dry landscape. "Maybe they won't see us if we stick to these trees."

"Yeah, right. There must be, what, three trees between us and them? They'll provide great cover," Joe said sarcastically. "I'm sure Daphne and Tracker will never notice the dust we're kicking up."

Frank ignored the comment, keeping his attention on the two vehicles in the distance. "Do you think they're in on the poaching together? I mean, why else would they meet out here in the middle of nowhere?"

"Beats me," Joe answered with a shrug. "If you're right, that would explain why we found her knife but no rifle in the gorge the other night. Maybe Tracker's the guy with the firepower."

"Daphne could have told Tracker ahead of time where we'd be camping," Harold added. He clutched the side of the Range Rover as it bounced over the scrub-covered earth. "After Tracker shot the night glider, she would have been on hand to—I don't know, distract us or something."

Looking ahead, Joe realized that Tracker and Daphne were only a few hundred yards in front of them. "Uh, Frank? We've gotten a lot closer. Maybe you should slow down before they see us."

Frank let up on the gas pedal and veered toward a gum tree to his right. But when Joe looked through the binoculars again, he saw Tracker and Daphne both turn their heads toward them. "Too late! They spotted us!" Joe exclaimed. The truck and the Range Rover took off. "Stay after them, Frank. If they're about to poach any wildlife, we can't afford to lose them."

Frank floored the gas, and they roared forward. To his right, Joe could see the road curving toward the gum trees at the main entrance to the national park. Daphne and Tracker were veering slightly west of there.

"There's a low ridge," Joe said, peering through the binoculars. "They're going to try to lose us behind it."

Sure enough, Daphne and Tracker disappeared behind the dusty brown rise. Frank poured on more speed, but it seemed like forever before they zoomed around the edge of the rise.

"I see them," Harold crowed, pointing.

Joe, too, had spotted the Range Rover winding through the scrub and trees a hundred yards ahead.

Frank jerked the wheel to the left, barely avoiding a large rock, and Joe slammed against the passenger door. "Watch it, Frank," he warned.

Up ahead, Tracker Jordan's truck screeched to the right and disappeared behind an outcropping of red rocks, Daphne right behind it.

"You haven't seen the last of us," Joe muttered.

When Frank got to the rocks, he jerked the wheel in a hard right and—

"Whoa!" Joe and Harold shouted at the same time.

Right in front of them was a huge swamp that stretched out in a ragged circle. They were headed for it at top speed.

"Brace yourselves!" Frank shouted, gripping the steering wheel. A second later the Rover plunged into the swamp, splashing warm brown water everywhere. The vehicle ground to a stop, throwing them all forward.

"Yee-oow!" Harold screamed.

"Are you two all right?" Joe asked.

"Fine," Frank muttered.

"I'll live," Harold said weakly. He was slumped forward over the front seat. As Harold lifted his head and gazed out over the muddy water, Joe saw fear come into his eyes.

"Oh, no!" Harold said. Suddenly all the color drained from his face. "Don't look now, but—"

"I know, I know. Daphne and Tracker got away," Joe finished, shaking his head in disgust. He could see two clouds of dust hugging the outer edge of the swamp, close to the ridge.

"No! That's not what I'm talking about!" Harold insisted. He sat back, jerked his feet up onto the seat, and clutched his metal camera case close to his body. "We've got to get out of here!"

Great, thought Joe. It was just their luck to get stuck out here with a guy who was afraid to get his sneakers smudged. He gazed out over the water. At first all he saw were a few dead branches and tree trunks arcing out of the water.

Then he spotted motionless round eyes and scaled snouts just sticking out of the water. They were so still that Joe had to look twice before he was sure of what they were.

"Crocs!" he gasped.

Chapter

Thirteen

W HAT!" Frank's mouth fell open when he spotted at least a dozen crocodiles heading toward them from all directions. They moved so slowly that the water barely rippled. "They're everywhere!"

"That's what I've been trying to tell you!" Harold squeaked out.

Feeling all those eyes on him made Frank shiver. "I don't know about you two, but I'm not planning on being tonight's dinner for those things."

"Me, neither." Joe looked around to gauge how far they were from the edge of the swamp. "It's only about eight feet. We've got to make a run for it now—before they get any closer."

Frank was already climbing into the backseat. "I thought I remembered seeing some rope back here." Triumphantly he grabbed it and held it up. Then, leaning over, he tied one end around the rear fender. "We can use this to pull the Rover out—I left it in neutral." He was about to jump when Harold grabbed his arm.

"We can't go in there. What if they get us?" Harold wailed.

"It's our only chance. If we stay here, they'll definitely get us," Frank said. "Now, come on." Harold just stared at him, panic in his eyes. Glancing over his shoulder, Frank saw that the closest crocodile was now just a few feet away.

"I hate to do this, but—Joe, take his arm." Frank grabbed Harold under one arm while Joe took the other. Before Harold could twist free, the brothers lifted him and pushed him out, sending him smack into the swampy brown water. While Harold floundered, trying to get his footing, Frank and Joe jumped in after him, with Frank keeping a tight grip on the free end of the rope. He didn't dare look behind him, but he could feel the crocodiles moving closer.

"Hurry!" Joe yelled, grabbing one of Harold's arms and dragging him toward dry land.

The next few seconds were some of the scariest in Frank's life. He didn't know how he and Joe did it, but at last they were out of the water. Frank started to run for the outcropping of red rocks, but Harold stopped him.

"Wait a minute—those aren't the dangerous kind," Harold said. He was staring through mud-splattered glasses at the crocodiles.

"Huh?" Joe turned and saw the crocodiles hovering in the water—they didn't show any signs of coming onto land.

"Those are freshwater crocs. They hardly ever attack humans," Harold explained. "They've got narrow smooth snouts and are only about eight or nine feet long. Salties are the dangerous kind. They've got stubby snouts and are much larger."

"Right," Frank said, starting to breathe more easily. His knuckles were white from gripping the rope so tightly. "In that case, we might as well get the Rover out of there."

Even though the Range Rover was in neutral, it took the three of them a half-hour to pull it out of the swamp. Then Frank and Joe walked around the wet, dripping vehicle to assess the damage.

"I don't think the water came up to the engine. Maybe it will start up," Joe said hopefully.

"Don't bother trying," Frank said. He pointed at the front right tire, which was wet, muddy, and completely flat. "We're not going anywhere until we change this tire."

"A flat?" Joe shot a worried glance westward. "By the time we change it, it'll be pitch-black."

The sun was just sinking below the horizon, Frank saw, sending ribbons of purple and red across the sky. He had been so focused on their chase that he hadn't noticed the clouds building or the vague dampness in the air. "This is just great," he said, sighing in frustration. "Daphne and Tracker got away, and we're stuck out here in the middle of nowhere with a flat tire. Is there anything else that could possibly go wrong?"

Just then a few drops of rain splatted on Frank's face. In a matter of seconds the rain grew heavier, soaking his hair and clothes.

"You had to ask, didn't you," Joe said, grimacing. Rivulets of water ran down his face and dripped from his chin. He went to the back of the Rover, where the spare was bolted into place, but the rain made it hard to loosen the bolt.

"Forget it," Frank said, wiping the rain from his face. "Look around, Joe. We're not going anywhere."

The heavy rain had turned the ground into a muddy river. Joe's eyes clouded over as he stared in the direction they'd come from. After a long moment he turned back to Frank. "I see a rocky overhang up there," he said, pointing. "It'll be drier there."

Harold looked back and forth between Frank and Joe. "You mean, sleep there?" he asked.

"The car's soaked," Joe pointed out. He started toward the rocks. "Come on. We might as well settle in."

"At least we've got each other for company," Harold put in, smiling at Frank.

Frank looked grimly out over the swamp. "The crocs, too. Let's not forget the crocs."

"'Airlie Beach Youth Hostel.'" Nancy read the neon sign that glowed in the darkening evening sky.

The sign hung over the doorway of a wooden bungalow just off the main road to Shute Harbour. Behind the bungalow, half a dozen cabins were set in what looked like a tropical garden. "It seems like ages since we booked our rooms here this morning," she said, smiling at Mick.

"Mmm." He smiled back, but Nancy didn't miss the underlying tension in his handsome face. It had been there all afternoon.

Mick had tried to enjoy himself while they snorkeled, but the beautiful fish and corals obviously hadn't been able to make him forget about the trouble Nellie was in. Nancy hadn't been able to relax, either.

After getting their keys from the registration desk, they headed for the cabins. "I'll meet you in the garden as soon as I shower and change," Nancy told Mick over her shoulder as she opened the door to the cabin she was sharing with three other girls.

Inside were four cots, a table, some shelves for personal items, and a small bathroom. After taking a quick shower, Nancy changed into jean shorts and a blue tank top, stowed her pack under her cot, then went out to meet Mick.

He was sitting on a bench among the garden's flowering bushes. When she joined him, Nancy saw the intense concentration on his face.

"Hi," she said quietly, sitting down next to him.

At first he didn't look at her. "You know, Nellie is one of the calmest, most decent people I've ever met," he said. "I've never seen her do anything rash or impetuous—it's just not like her. I know you must think she's unstable, but you have to believe me—she would never run like this unless something was terribly wrong."

Nancy's heart went out to him. "She seems like a really good person," she said truthfully. "I know we'll get to the bottom of what's going on soon."

Mick's eyes softened as he glanced at her. "I'm sorry, Nancy."

"I'm not. I'm glad to do anything I can to help Nellie," Nancy said.

"I guess I just hoped that somehow . . ." He hesitated, staring hard into Nancy's eyes, then turned brusquely away. "Never mind."

"What?" Nancy was breathless. The way he had looked at her—she felt as if he'd seen straight through her.

Mick took a deep breath before turning to her again. "It's just that I feel so . . . close to you. Can you really tell me you don't feel the same way about me?"

"Yes—I mean, no—" Nancy tried to sort through the jumble of emotions she was feeling. "Haven't we been through all this before?"

"Mmm. But it seems to me we still have a lot to work out." Mick tipped her chin up and gave Nancy a long kiss that left her tingling from head to toe. Before she had time to think about what was happening, however, a girl's voice spoke up behind her.

"Excuse me. You are Nancy Drew?"

Nancy pulled back from Mick, feeling her face grow hot. A girl about her own age was standing a few feet away. "Yes, I'm Nancy."

"I'm sharing your cabin," the girl explained. Judging by her accent, Nancy guessed she was from one of the Scandinavian countries. "Irene, the woman at the desk, asked me to give this to you."

The girl held out a package wrapped in brown paper. "Thanks," Nancy said, taking it. As the girl walked toward their cabin, Nancy examined the block letters spelling out her name.

"Who could be sending you something here?" Mick wondered aloud.

"There's only one way to find out." Nancy tore the paper open, then lifted the lid of the cardboard box inside.

"What?" She was staring down at a rubber snake, its body coiled for attack. It was more grotesque than scary, but beside the snake was a note that chilled Nancy to the bone: NEXT TIME YOU WON'T BE SO LUCKY.

Chapter

Fourteen

I DON'T BELIEVE THIS!" Mick said. He took the note from Nancy and stared at it grimly. "Someone is really trying to get us off the case."

"Yes, but who?" Nancy asked. "It has to be someone who knew that we'd be staying here *and* someone who knew about the taipan in my pack."

"Gil is the only person who knows we're here," Mick pointed out.

Nancy frowned, trying to think through the possibilities. "Yes," she said slowly, "but how could he have known about the taipan? Besides, I don't see why he'd do this."

"Someone who doesn't want us to find Nellie, then," Mick suggested. "The person who planted the taipan in your pack must have followed us back here."

"Maybe." Nancy had thought of another possibility, too, but she knew Mick wasn't going to like it. "Or it might have been Nellie herself." She held up a hand to stop Mick's protest. "I agree that it doesn't sound like her, but running away from us at the harbor didn't seem like her, either."

Mick jerked to his feet and started to pace in front of the bench. "This is awful. I don't know what to do or whom to trust anymore."

Nancy knew how he felt. It seemed as if the more they investigated, the more confused things became. With every minute that passed, Nellie could be in more danger, but she didn't want their help. Nancy just hoped they could find Nellie before her time ran out for good.

The first thing Joe was aware of when he woke up was his growling stomach. The second was a deafening assortment of squawks and chirps echoing around him.

"Hey, will someone turn down that nature show?" he mumbled sleepily. It wasn't until he tried to pull his nonexistent pillow over his head and his hand hit something rock hard instead that he remembered where he was. Slowly, he cracked open one eye, then groaned as it all came back to him. The swamp, the crocodiles, the rain . . .

"It's about time you woke up," Frank said.

Joe pushed himself to a sitting position, then blinked in amazement as he looked down from the rock ledge. The sun shone brightly over the muddy outback. The rain had swelled the swamp into a small lake that came to within a few feet of the bottom of the rocks where they'd slept. Hundreds of birds, kangaroos, and other animals waded in the water or perched in the nearby trees. Frank and Harold were both standing at the edge of the water in their muddy, wrinkled clothes, looking up at him.

Joe groaned when his gaze fell on the Range Rover. They had pulled it to dry land the day before, but the rain had caused the swamp to spread so much that now it encircled the vehicle again. The murky, brown water came up to the tops of the tires. Two spoonbills were standing on the hood, while smaller birds perched along the windshield.

"You two look about as lousy as I feel," Joe said.

"Not at all!" Harold said brightly. He tapped the camera around his neck. "Luckily this is waterproof. I've been getting fantastic photos."

"Well, at least one of us is happy. Do you think there's anything out here we can eat?" Joe asked as his stomach growled again. He stretched, then climbed down to Frank and Harold, causing the birds near them to scatter with loud shrieks.

"I'm sure we can dig up a few witchetty grubs," Frank said with a grin. "Otherwise, we'll have to wait until we get the car out of there and change the flat."

"I think I'll skip the worms, thanks," Joe said, grimacing. He scrutinized the water's surface. "At least the crocs seem to be keeping a low profile. We might as well get to work."

Frank rolled his eyes at the Rover. "I can't believe we didn't think to pull it farther from the edge of the water yesterday. I should have realized that downpour would swell the swamp. Well, at least the rope is still tied to the fender." He raised an eyebrow at Harold and Joe. "Any volunteers to wade out there and evict those birds?"

"Don't hurt them," Harold put in quickly. "Those spoonbills are real beauts. And those smaller yellow, white, and blue birds are sulphur-crested cockatoos."

"Don't worry," Joe assured him. Harold hadn't exactly jumped at the chance to wade out, he noticed. Taking a last look around for crocodiles, Joe waded into the muddy water himself.

"I'll steer while you guys use the rope to pull me out," he said over his shoulder. "If we're lucky, maybe the engine will start."

As Joe approached the Rover, more birds scattered, squawking loudly. He climbed over the door, then sat behind the wheel and turned the key that dangled from the ignition. "Come on," he muttered under his breath as the engine chugged. Finally it sputtered and caught.

"All right!" Joe crowed. "We'll have this baby out of here in no time."

"This is taking forever!" Joe burst out, banging his hands against the steering wheel.

That was the understatement of the year, as far as Frank was concerned. They'd been trying to get their Range Rover out of the swampy water for the last hour. He and Harold had taken turns searching for pieces of wood to wedge beneath the tires, but nothing had worked. So far, all they had to show for their efforts were blisters and even muddier clothes than before. They had all taken off their shirts, but Frank was still sweating, and he was going deaf listening to Joe gun the engine.

Gritting his teeth, Frank clenched the rope for what seemed like the millionth time. "Hit it, Joe!"

The engine roared, but the wheels spun uselessly in the muddy water. Even with Frank and Harold putting all their strength into pulling the rope, the Range Rover wouldn't budge.

"I give up!" Harold exclaimed, dropping the rope. He wiped his red, sweaty face with the back of his hand. "We're not getting anywhere. I'd better look for something bigger to lodge under the wheels."

As Harold disappeared behind some thick brush at the swamp's edge, Frank turned to his brother. "Let's face it, Joe. This isn't working—Joe?"

His brother had turned around, but he was peering behind Frank. "Hear that?" Joe asked.

It was the sound of an engine. Frank heard it coming closer, and a minute later Tracker Jordan's pickup appeared around the outcrop of red rocks. "What's he doing here?" Frank muttered.

Tracker stopped his truck, got out, leaned against the hood, and crossed his arms over his chest. "Looks like you city boys are in a bit of trouble," he said, a taunting smile on her face.

"No thanks to you," Frank said, glaring at Tracker.

"Why are you here?" Joe demanded. "You and Daphne didn't kill enough animals yesterday, so you came back for more?"

"If you say so," Tracker answered. There was an amused glint in his eyes. Frank couldn't tell if he was joking or not. "I thought you three might be needing a hand."

The guy's cocky attitude was starting to rub Frank the wrong way. "We don't need your kind of help, pal," he said, but Tracker didn't seem to be listening. He walked over to Frank, took the rope, and tied it to his truck's front fender. Then he got back in his truck and called out the window, "Okay, hit the gas!"

As Tracker started backing up his truck, Joe shrugged at Frank. Then he gunned the engine. At first the tires didn't catch. The rope was so taut, Frank was afraid it might snap. Then the Range Rover took a sudden jump back toward the edge of the swamp.

Tracker continued backing up until the Range Rover was out of the water. Then he stopped and got out to untie the rope. As he handed it back to Frank, he said, "You boys should think twice before you head into the outback on your own. It can be a dangerous place." Then he simply strode back to his truck and drove away.

"Hey! What happened?" Harold asked, reappearing from behind the brush with a thick log. He seemed surprised to see the Range Rover sitting on dry ground. "How'd you get unstuck? Who was that?"

Frank frowned. "Tracker Jordan pulled the Rover out with his truck. Either he felt like gloating, or he felt guilty about getting us stuck."

"Or he's up to no good," Joe put in. He gestured at the riotous birds all around them. "This swamp would be a gold mine to a poacher."

Frank's eyes narrowed as he looked around. "Well, we're not exactly in a position to do anything about it at the moment. We'll be lucky if we make it back to Gil's in all this mud."

"Plus, we've still got to change that flat," Joe said. He stepped over to the deflated front right tire and kicked it in frustration.

It took the three of them another fifteen minutes to change the tire. When they were finally ready to go, Frank walked over to get his shirt from the bush where he'd thrown it earlier. "Hey!" He stopped, peering at the ground several yards behind the bush. "You guys, I think I see blood."

"What!" Joe exclaimed. "Where?"

Frank was already jogging toward the spot. Sure enough, the muddy earth was pitted with small pools of blood. "Looks like tracks," he said as Joe and Harold caught up to him.

"I don't like this," Joe muttered grimly. He, Frank, and Harold followed the pitted tracks to a small shrub. Frank gently separated the blood-spattered leaves of the bush—then gasped.

A bird was shivering under the branches of the bush. It was about a foot long, with a pale blue tail and a plume of yellow at the back of its head. The rest of the bird was white—except for the circle of blood that covered one snowy wing.

"That's a sulphur-crested cockatoo!" Harold exclaimed in dismay. "It's been wounded."

"We've got to help it," Frank said. He started to reach for the cockatoo but hesitated when the bird started squawking and flapping its wings frantically.

"Don't make any sudden moves," Harold whispered. "You'll only scare it into hurting itself even more."

Frank and Joe stood completely still. "What should we do?" Frank asked, his voice low and calm. "How long do you think it's been bleeding?"

"Not too long—it's still fairly alert." Harold began talking to the bird in a soothing voice. At the same time he slowly took Frank's shirt from him. "I'm not going to hurt you."

Very slowly he moved closer to the cockatoo, holding out Frank's shirt by the tail. The bird was shaking, but at least it wasn't moving around in a panic anymore. The creature seemed mesmerized by Harold's actions. When Harold came within reach of the bird, he scooped it up.

"There we go," he said in the same calm voice. In one quick motion he deftly wrapped the shirt around the creature so that the wounded wing was pressed close against its body.

"Not bad," Frank complimented him.

"This bird needs help," Harold said, gently cradling the cockatoo in his hands.

"Let's go back to town," Joe said. "Someone there must know what to do."

Frank held the passenger door open for Harold and then hopped into the backseat.

"Joe?" he called into the brush. "Come on. We've got to hurry."

"Sorry," Joe said, jogging up. "I got distracted when I found this." He tossed something small and metallic to Frank, then climbed behind the wheel.

Frank guessed what it was even before he caught it. "A shell casing," he said, turning it over in his palm. "Exactly like the one we found in the national park near the yellow-bellied glider."

"No big surprise there," Joe said, starting the engine. "The ten-million-dollar question is, Who's the shooter? And why is he always striking wherever *we* are?"

Negotiating the muddy terrain wasn't easy, and for a few minutes no one said anything. As the sounds of birds faded behind them, Joe turned around briefly to Frank.

"Think Tracker Jordan did it?" Joe suggested. "He could have shot the cockatoo while we were trying to get unstuck. The way I was revving the engine, it's no wonder we didn't hear the shot."

"I'm not sure," Frank said, shaking his head. "I mean, if you were going around killing rare animals, wouldn't you avoid doing it when other people were around? Jordan could have waited until after we left to shoot the cockatoo."

"I'm quite glad he didn't," Harold said angrily. "If he had, he might have succeeded in killing this exquisite creature."

Joe met Frank's eyes in the rearview mirror. "But if it wasn't Jordan, then who?"

Frank shrugged distractedly, then said, "The way the shooter keeps striking near us, it's almost as if he's taunting us. Or trying to scare us off."

"Or she," Joe put in. "Daphne could have shot the bird while Tracker was helping us. I bet anything they're in this together, working for Dennis Moore."

Frank sighed. "I can't think about this on an empty stomach," he said as his stomach growled yet again. "Let's get back to Flat Hill so we can eat."

"Here we are," Mick announced at Shute Harbour Wednesday morning. "I hope we have better luck today than we did yesterday."

"Me, too," Nancy agreed. "It takes a lot more than a threatening note and a rubber snake to scare me off a case." Nancy did know that she and Mick would have to be very careful from now on, though.

She squinted toward the row of warehouses and offices across from the harbor. The hot morning sun glared off the buildings, making it hard to see clearly. "That's the building we saw Nellie come out of, isn't it?" she asked, pointing toward one of the glass storefronts.

Mick shaded his eyes from the sun. "Yeah. Let's check it out."

He was already striding across the street. As Nancy followed, she noticed the sign next to the building's glass entrance. "Branden Developers," she murmured. As she got closer to the building, she saw a poster taped to the inside of the door, advertising a condominium complex on one of the Whitsunday Islands.

Mick was waiting for Nancy next to the door. "This makes no sense to me," he said, flicking a thumb toward the poster. "Nellie couldn't buy a condo. Why would she come here?"

"Let's find out," Nancy said, and pulled open the door.

"Looks like no one's home," Mick said.

Inside the office were two desks, each outfitted with a computer and chairs for customers. The desks were empty, but through an open doorway behind one of the desks, Nancy heard someone talking on the phone.

"If I've said it once, I've said it a thousand times," a man's voice spoke sharply. "I don't care about the girl! If she's in the way, take care of her."

Nancy saw the way Mick tensed up at the mention of "the girl." He pressed a finger to his lips.

"No more excuses," the man went on. "You promised me opals—top-quality black opals."

Opals! Nancy froze. She was almost afraid to breathe for fear of missing the man's next words. When he spoke again, his voice had a cold, steely edge to it that made her shiver.

"Tell your sob story to someone who cares. We made a deal, and you'd better deliver—or else."

Chapter
Fifteen

A MOMENT LATER Nancy heard the man bang the telephone receiver into its cradle and mutter something under his breath. Before she had time to think about what to do, he strode through the doorway. In his forties, the man had short black hair, a wide face, and a barrel-chested build that reminded Nancy of a boxer's. He wore light-colored slacks and a white polo shirt that set off his even tan. When he saw Nancy and Mick, he stopped midstride, surprise and irritation on his face.

"Oh—I didn't realize anyone was here," he said. His eyes narrowed, and Nancy had the impression he was trying to gauge how much they had overheard.

"Hi! My, uh, fiancé and I just stepped in. We

were afraid no one was here," Nancy said quickly, shooting Mick a look that said to play along.

The man seemed to relax the slightest bit. "Is there something I can help you with?" he asked.

"We were admiring the poster for your Paradise Cove condos," Nancy improvised, recalling the name on the poster. She didn't really care about the resort, but she wanted to get this man talking. "Could you tell us about the development, Mr.—"

The man eyed her and Mick dubiously before answering. "Branden. Clyde Branden," he said slowly. "Aren't you two a little young to be investing in real estate?"

"It's never too early to start planning for the future," Mick put in quickly. Slipping an arm around Nancy's shoulders, he gave Branden a wide smile.

"We've already heard a little about Paradise Cove," Nancy added brightly. "A friend of ours was raving about it."

"Oh?" The developer seemed to be losing interest. He gestured vaguely to one of the desks and said, "My sales representative should be in shortly. You can talk to her—"

"Perhaps you remember meeting our friend," Mick cut in, picking up on Nancy's comment. "Nellie Mabo?"

Nancy didn't miss the sudden spark of suspicion in Clyde Branden's eyes, but all he said was, "No, I don't think so."

"She's an Aborigine girl, about so high," Mick went on, indicating Nellie's height with one hand.

"Usually wears a scarf in her hair." He gave Nancy's shoulders a squeeze. "Honey, didn't she say she spoke to the owner?"

"Must have been someone else," Branden said curtly before Nancy could answer. "I'm very busy. You two will have to come back when my sales rep is here."

Nancy knew they had struck a nerve. Branden started ushering them toward the door, but Nancy resisted. "Perhaps you could help us with one more thing?"

"What?" Branden asked, giving an irritated sigh. He wasn't even trying to be polite anymore.

"I'd like to buy some opals, but my fiancé isn't from this part of Australia. Do you know if there's a good shop in the area?"

Nancy waited for his reaction, and she wasn't disappointed. Beneath his tan, Branden's face seemed to darken. "I'm in the real estate business, not gem trading," he spat out. His angry gaze shot back and forth between Nancy and Mick. "I think you two have wasted enough of my time. G'day." With that, he opened the door and gestured for them to leave.

After they had crossed back over to the harbor, Mick turned to Nancy. "He definitely recognized Nellie's description," he said excitedly. "And did you hear him talking about black opals?"

Nancy nodded. "We can't be sure he was talking about the same ones that were stolen from the Royces, but he was definitely acting suspiciously."

"Branden said something about a girl interfering. That could be Nellie," Mick added. There was a troubled glimmer in his eyes as he sat down on a bench. "He sounded as if he meant it when he told the other person to take care of her."

"Maybe Nellie somehow got in the way of whoever stole the opals, and that's why she's on the run," Nancy said, thinking out loud. "But we still don't know who the thief is or what Clyde Branden may have had to do with Nellie's disappearance."

"I don't think we can count on Branden to give us any answers, either," Mick added grimly.

"Maybe not voluntarily, but there are other ways of getting information," Nancy said, raising an eyebrow at him.

"What are you suggesting—that we kidnap Branden and hang him by his thumbs until he confesses?"

"Nothing that drastic," Nancy said with a laugh. "I was thinking more along the lines of staking out his office and following him. We definitely made him nervous just now."

"Maybe nervous enough to give away what he's up to," Mick finished. He stood up and dug into his jeans pocket for some change. "I'm going to try to track down George at Flat Hill. Find out what progress she's made. I'll meet you back here."

"Good idea," Nancy told him. "If I'm not here when you get back, it means I've followed Branden. If that happens, we'll meet back at the hostel."

"Good," he said, then headed off.

Nancy turned her attention to the office, hoping this lead wasn't another dead end.

"I hope Gil is back," Joe said, parking the Range Rover in front of the Outback Adventures office. "How's our friend doing, Harold?"

Joe had been so busy navigating the muddy roads that he hadn't been able to pay much attention to the wounded cockatoo. Now he noticed that there was a bloodstain on Frank's shirt where it covered the wounded wing. The bird shivered in Harold's hands.

"At least it's still alive," Frank commented. Joe was half a step behind the other two when they stepped into the Outback Adventures office. Daphne was sitting at Gil's desk, beneath a poster for Outback Adventures. She looked up in surprise from the ledger she was bent over.

"What happened to you guys? You look as if you ran into a mudslide." She broke off as her gaze fell on the cockatoo in Harold's hands. "Oh! The poor thing is wounded."

She jumped up, ran over, and gently took the bird from Harold. She unwound the shirt to examine the terrified bird. When she saw the bloodied wing, she frowned darkly. "It's been shot." There was a mixture of outrage and surprise in her voice. Turning to Frank and Joe, she guessed, "The poacher?"

Frank nodded. "You might ask your friend Tracker Jordan about the details," he said.

For a split second Daphne froze. Giving him an uneasy glance, she said, "Look, about yesterday—"

"Save the excuses," Joe cut in sharply. "We all know you two were up to no good. You've just been lucky enough not to get caught so far."

"What!" As she glared at him, Joe could see the defensive wall go up between them. She clamped her mouth shut and reached for a first-aid kit that was on the wall behind the desk.

Watching her disinfect and wrap the bird's wound, Joe wasn't sure what to think. Daphne seemed so surprised and distressed about the cockatoo, it was hard to imagine that she could be involved in the poaching. Then again, what had her knife been doing so near the dead night glider? And why would she lie about its not being hers? Not to mention that she and Tracker had purposely gotten them stuck in that swamp, soon after Daphne had spoken to Dennis Moore.

Daphne Whooten was definitely hiding something. And sooner or later Joe and Frank would find out what.

"You two look almost human again," Gil Strickland said as Joe came into Gil's living room.

Joe shook his wet hair and glanced down at the clean jeans and T-shirt he'd just put on. "I might start to feel human again, too, as soon as I get something to eat. It's after ten, and we haven't eaten since yesterday afternoon."

"Tell me about it," Frank put in. He had taken a

shower before Joe and was sitting on the couch flipping through a magazine. "My stomach has been growling so much I'm beginning to think I swallowed a small motor."

"I don't have much in the way of eats," Gil said apologetically. "I thought I'd be out hiking with my clients. Haven't had a chance to stock up since I got back from the coast last night."

"It stinks that they canceled on you," Joe said.

Gil nodded soberly. "When I got to Mackay, the couple told me they'd decided to stay at the beach," he explained. "They paid for the flight, but"—he frowned and gazed out the window—"I could use the money they were going to pay me for taking them bush walking."

Just then the kitchen telephone rang, and Gil got up to answer it. "Hello?" He frowned as he listened, then burst out, "What!"

Uh-oh, thought Joe. Sounds like more bad news.

"Yes, of course. I can be there in a few hours," Gil went on. He listened some more, then said, "I'm sure your trip here will be time well spent. . . . Yes, of course. See you then."

Gil hung up the phone, then turned to Frank and Joe. "If we're going to get a bite to eat, we'd better make it fast. I've got to turn around and fly back to Whitsunday."

"Another client?" Frank guessed.

Gil nodded. "Too bad I didn't know about this before I flew back here last night," he said. "But I can use the business. With any luck, my money problems will be over soon." As he spoke, he headed for his bedroom. "It'll take just a minute to get together what I need. You two can fill me in on your investigation while we eat. Call it a late breakfast for you and an early lunch for me. I'll leave for my plane from there."

At the Flat Hill Lodge, Frank and Joe parked right behind Gil. As they walked inside, the Hardys quickly told Gil about finding the knife sheath at Daphne's and about what had happened at the swamp. "We saw her talking to Dennis Moore, too," Frank finished as they entered the restaurant. "Maybe it was an innocent conversation, but when I asked her about it, she wouldn't tell me what he wanted."

"Daphne? A poacher? No way," Gil said emphatically as they sat down.

Joe wasn't surprised by Gil's reaction. It had to be a shock for him to consider Daphne a suspect. "What about her rendezvous with Tracker Jordan?" he asked. "They deliberately got us stuck in that swamp."

"It doesn't make sense to me," Gil insisted. "I've never heard them talk much to each other, except to trade insults."

"You have to admit she's been acting suspiciously," Joe said. After glancing at the menu, he added, "I think I'll have one of everything. I'm starved."

Before long they were digging into plates heaped with steak, eggs, and fried potatoes. Joe cleared his plate in record time. He was thinking about ordering another steak when George burst into the restaurant.

"Frank! Joe!" she exclaimed. "Boy, am I glad to see you guys." She hurried over to them, carrying a flat package wrapped in brown paper.

"What's up?" Frank asked. He lowered his voice before adding, "Any new leads on your case?"

"I'm not sure." George plunked the package down on the table. "This just came for Mick. The postman said he found it outside the post office a few days ago. It didn't have any stamps, but he decided to deliver it anyway. Do you think I should open it? I mean, what if it's something that could help us find Nellie?"

The package was addressed to Mick in care of Nellie's trailer, Joe saw. "I say check it out. Mick will understand."

"Be careful. We can't be sure it isn't booby-trapped," Frank cautioned. He picked up the package and gently felt around the sealed flap. George, Joe, and Gil all leaned forward while Frank carefully opened the wrinkled paper and pulled out what appeared to be an oblong piece of bark about six inches by ten inches. Simple lines and shapes had been carved into it.

"A bark carving," Gil said, tracing the lines with his finger. "It was done recently."

"I bet Nellie did it!" George exclaimed. She looked excitedly around the table. "You guys, I think Nellie's trying to send us a message."

Chapter

Sixteen

"Are you sure?" Frank took the bark carving from George and studied it. "You mean, these symbols stand for things?"

"Definitely," George answered. "It's like a map. I'm not sure exactly what it all means, but Nellie said that the lines represent a person's path, and the circles are campsites or other places."

Picking up the carving, Gil stared at it closely. "I know a little about the Aboriginal symbols," he said. "Maybe I can help you out."

"It looks as if there are other symbols, too," Frank said, looking over Gil's shoulder. "Is that some kind of animal—" He broke off as someone whisked the bark carving away from him. "Hey!"

Standing next to their table was an Aborigine man with dark curly hair and a mustache. He clutched the carving and glared at Frank. "You have no right to handle this," the man snapped.

"Someone sent this to Mick, Mr. Whiteair," George explained. "We think it was Nellie." Apparently, George had met this guy before, but Frank didn't get the feeling they were buddies.

"This is a traditional aboriginal artifact," Yami said, biting off the words. "You are trying to steal it from my people, the way you have stolen everything else."

"We didn't steal anything," George objected. "I'm telling you, Nellie sent it to Mick." She picked up the paper with Mick's name printed on it, but it was too late. Yami was storming out of the restaurant with the carving.

"Jeez! Talk about touchy," Joe commented, shaking his head. "Who was that guy?"

"Yami Whiteair. He was around when we found the tjuringa," George explained. "He's very protective of the Yungis' traditions. He thinks Nellie shouldn't have anything to do with people who aren't Aborigines."

Gil stared at Yami's retreating figure. "He has good reason to be protective. Aborigines have had to fight hard for their legal rights here."

"That doesn't change the fact that the bark carving was sent to Mick, not Yami," Frank said. "He didn't have any right to take it. How can we find out what Nellie was trying to say?"

George took the paper the carving had been wrapped in and crumpled it in her fingers. "It's weird," she began, her brow furrowed. "The other day, Yami Whiteair said something about how the Yungis should just take what's rightfully theirs because they're always getting shafted by the legal system."

"Like their fight with Royce Mining?" Joe inquired.

"Exactly," George answered. "I didn't think anything of it at the time, but now . . ." She hesitated a moment, then said, "Maybe he took that carving because he's afraid there's something in it that implicates him in the opal theft."

"You think he might have stolen the opals as a way of taking back what the Yungis deserve?" Frank asked.

"Maybe," George answered. "I know it's a long shot, but I don't know if we can afford to ignore it."

"Why don't you tell Nellie's grandfather what happened?" Frank suggested.

George nodded slowly. "Good idea. He's a leader of the tribe. If anyone can convince Yami Whiteair to let us examine the bark carving, he can."

"Well, that was a bust," Joe said forty-five minutes later as he, Frank, and George walked back into the Flat Hill Lodge.

"So much for the amazing persuasive powers of crack detectives," George added. "Mr. Mabo wouldn't even talk to us."

Joe didn't blame her for being upset. When they'd gone to Mr. Mabo's house, he'd refused to let them in, saying that the Yungis' lawyer had recommended that they not speak to anyone without consulting him first.

"That makes our job harder," George said. "I wish there was some way to get in touch with Nancy and Mick."

"Gil said they were staying in some hostel in Airlie Beach," Frank said. "Is there a phone book here for that part of Australia?"

The registration desk was empty, but there was a bell on the counter and a small sign that read Ring for Service. Frank rang, and a lanky middle-aged man appeared through a curtained doorway behind the counter. As Frank was asking for a phone book, the phone on the counter rang. "Hello?" the man answered. "You're wanting to speak with whom? George Fame?"

"George *Fayne,*" George corrected, jumping forward. "That's me."

"Finally," the man said. He plucked a handful of messages from behind the desk and pushed them toward George. "This bloke's been leaving messages for you for the past hour."

George took the receiver the man offered. "Hello? Mick! We were just trying to call you."

Frank listened while George told Mick about the bark carving. After talking to him for a few minutes, she hung up and turned back to Frank and Joe. "Mick thinks the carving could be important, too," she told them. "It's barely noon. He says they might be able to hook up with Gil so they can fly back with him today."

"Did they have any luck finding Nellie?" Joe asked.

"They spotted her, but she got away from them," George answered. "They still don't know why, but maybe there's an explanation in that bark carving. If Mick can convince Mr. Whiteair and Mr. Mabo to tell us what the carving means, we might be able to make sense of what's been happening."

Nancy glanced at her watch, then turned her attention back to the Branden Developers office. It was twelve o'clock. In the hour since Mick had left to call George, the building had been quiet. Clyde Branden hadn't left, and the only person to enter was a young woman wearing a suit. Nancy guessed she was the sales representative Branden had mentioned.

The hot sun was beating down. Even in the shade, Nancy felt beads of perspiration pop out on her forehead. If Clyde Branden was going to make a move, she hoped he would do it soon.

Just then a flicker of motion inside the glass door caught her attention. The door swung open, and Clyde Branden stepped outside. Judging from the nervous way he glanced around, Nancy guessed that he wasn't taking a lunch break.

Now we're in business, she thought. She hunched down low on the bench until he started walking toward the harbor parking lot. Then she followed at a distance. As soon as she saw him unlock a gray sedan, she waved for a taxi from the line waiting at the edge of the harbor.

"Follow that gray car," she said, jumping into the taxi's backseat. "The one that's about to leave the parking lot."

The driver gave her a sideways glance. "What is this, some kind of spy movie?"

"Please, it's important," Nancy urged.

With a shrug, the driver pulled into the heavy traffic. "Whatever you say, miss."

Branden's sedan was half a dozen cars ahead of theirs. Nancy leaned forward, keeping her eyes glued to it. "Up there. He's turning left."

"I got eyes," the driver said. But Nancy was relieved to see that he picked up his speed once they took the turn. They were just two cars behind the sedan now. Branden didn't seem to be in any hurry—he probably hadn't noticed her. Nancy relaxed a little and sat back. They were heading into a residential neighborhood. Could Branden be heading for his home?

Nancy bolted upright. The gray sedan was cruising through an intersection on the yellow. "That light is about to turn red! Hurry, or we'll miss it!"

The driver shook his head as he slowed to a stop. "I've never gotten a ticket, and I don't plan to start now," he said, glancing at her over his shoulder. "Sorry, miss."

Nancy let out a groan as the sedan turned right at the next corner. "This is just great," she muttered. "We've lost him." By now, Mick might have already returned, and when he found out she'd left, he would probably go back to their hostel to wait for her.

"Miss?" The light had turned green, Nancy realized, and the driver was looking at her expectantly. "Where to now?"

Stifling her frustration, she told the driver, "The Airlie Beach Youth Hostel, please."

When she got to the hostel, Nancy went first to the reception bungalow. Irene was standing behind the counter, flipping through a tabloid. She smiled when she saw Nancy. "Ah! Good, you're here," she said cheerfully. "Your friend left just a few minutes ago."

"Mick? Where did he go?"

Irene shrugged. "All I know is he took his things and asked me to give you this as soon as you showed up."

Nancy took the note the older woman handed her and quickly opened it: "Important news from George. We've got to return to Flat Hill, ASAP. Meet me at the Whitsunday Airport—cargo hangar." Mick had signed the note with just an *M*.

"Bad news?" Irene inquired.

Nancy realized that she was frowning. Dozens of questions ran through her mind, but she didn't have time to think about them now. "I don't think so," she told Irene. She folded the note, then slipped it into her pocket. "I've got to check out right away. And I'll need a taxi to the airport."

The next ten minutes went by in a flurry. It wasn't until Nancy was sitting in the backseat of another taxi that she let herself think about what was going on. She didn't feel good about leaving Airlie Beach without finding Nellie or discovering what Clyde Branden was up to. Why did George want them to return to Flat Hill? Had she found out who the opal thief was? Had some other crime taken place? Not only that, but how were they going to get back to the outback? As far as she knew, Gil had returned the day before.

By the time the taxi pulled up to the cargo hangar at Airlie Beach, it was almost one. Nancy's taxi wound around a small building for commercial flights to a strip of airplane hangars that ran alongside the landing strips. Mick was standing next to his backpack in front of the second hangar they passed.

"There," Nancy directed the taxi driver, pointing. She could see Gil inside the hangar, bent over the engine of his plane. Nancy paid the fare, then jumped out of the taxi. "Mick! I got your message. What's so important that—"

"Honey," Mick called, jogging over to Nancy. There was a big smile on his face, and his voice was falsely bright. Something was up. "I'm so happy to see you."

Nancy wasn't at all prepared for what happened next. Mick bent close and covered her mouth in a kiss that sent a delicious shiver through her body. When he finally pulled away, she felt dazed.

"What?"

Mick held a finger to her lips. Then in the same, too-bright voice he'd used before, he said, "Sweetheart, you'll never guess who's coming to Flat Hill with us."

Nancy blinked, trying to make sense of what was

happening. She gazed over Mick's shoulder into the hangar again. Gil was still bent over the engine, but now another person stepped out from behind the plane.

"I don't believe it," she whispered. "It's Clyde Branden!"

Chapter

Seventeen

Nancy had never been so confused in her life. "What's he doing here?" she asked in a whisper.

There was no time for Mick to answer. Clyde Branden was already coming their way.

"Well, well," Branden said, sauntering up to Nancy and Mick. "Isn't this a coincidence?" He smiled at Nancy, but the expression in his eyes was anything but friendly.

"It sure is," Nancy replied. She plastered a smile on her own face, then asked, "Do you have business in Flat Hill?" She wondered if Branden's trip had anything to do with the important development Mick had mentioned in his note.

"No, this is strictly a pleasure trip," Branden answered.

"Mr. Branden decided he's been working too

hard," Gil put in. He wiped his hands on a rag as he stepped up to the group. "Well, you've chosen the right vacation. There's nothing like a hike into the bush to take a man's mind off business."

"Mmm." Nancy eyed Gil nervously. What if he had mentioned their case to Branden, not knowing the developer might be involved? Had Mick been able to alert Gil to the story they had given Clyde Branden? If not, they could be in big trouble.

A moment later Gil gave her a secret wink that put her mind to rest. "Your fiancé tells me you're interested in buying some opals while you're in the outback," he said.

"Yes," Nancy said, relieved. At least her cover wasn't broken. Now, if she could just find out what was going on. "Honey, can you help me stow my things?" she asked Mick.

As they walked to the plane, Mick bent close to her. "Nellie sent me a bark carving, but Yami Whiteair intercepted it," he explained in a rushed whisper. "We have to get back right away to try to convince Yami and Mr. Mabo to show it to us."

"But how—" Nancy fell silent when she heard Gil and Clyde Branden coming up behind them. There wouldn't be any opportunity to talk privately in Gil's tiny propeller plane. Her questions would have to wait until they were back at Flat Hill.

"What! The bark carving is gone?" Mick stared at Mr. Mabo in disbelief. "How is that possible?"

It was late afternoon, and he and Nancy had just arrived. They had decided that it might be better not to show up with an army of people, so George had stayed in town with the Hardys.

As Nancy stepped into the house, she was surprised to see that Yami Whiteair was already there, sitting at the wooden table in the front room. "I'm confused," she said. "What did you do with the carving?"

Yami eyed Nancy and Mick suspiciously as they sat down with him and Nellie's grandfather at the table. When he said nothing, Mick turned to Mr. Mabo. "Can you tell us what happened?"

Nellie's grandfather gave a slow nod. "After your friends came, I wanted to see this carving for myself. I know my granddaughter. If the carving was really from her, I would recognize it."

"And?" Nancy prompted.

"I went with Yami to his home, where he had left the carving," Mr. Mabo continued. "When we got there"—he wiggled his fingers lightly in the air—"it had melted into nothing."

Nancy exchanged a sober look with Mick. "A bark carving couldn't just disappear. Someone had to take it," she said.

"Who?" Mick wondered aloud. Nancy saw the wary glance he gave Yami. The man hadn't been very cooperative. Was it simply that he didn't trust anyone outside the Yungi community, or did he have something to hide?

"I know what you are thinking," Yami said, meeting Mick's gaze. "Your eyes have questions but no trust."

"You have to trust us, too," Nancy said earnestly.

"We're trying to help find Nellie and clear her name. She could be in danger."

Yami looked at them for a long moment. "I wish Nellie no harm," he said at last. "Her carving . . . I did not look closely, but I could try to re-create the symbols."

Nellie's grandfather nodded approvingly. He got up from the table, went into the back room, and returned with a pencil and paper, which he gave to Yami. In a matter of seconds the paper had become a map of circles, dots, lines, and other markings.

"Nellie's told me a little about the symbols," Mick commented. "Those squiggly lines represent some kind of water, right?"

"Yes," Nellie's grandfather answered. "That is Comet Creek, running through the gorges. And that circle is the Flat Hill."

Pointing to a grid of circles next to the rock, Nancy asked, "And is this the town?"

Yami nodded. "There were some other symbols . . . some of the animals. And I think there was something special in the town of Flat Hill—I cannot remember exactly what."

"That's okay," Nancy told him. "This is already a big help." She and Mick bent over the drawing, but Yami got to his feet. He nodded to Nellie's grandfather before heading for the door.

"Yami must prepare for tonight's corroboree," Mr. Mabo explained to Nancy and Mick.

"That's right!" Mick exclaimed. "I forgot all about the dance."

"You will be there?" Mr. Mabo asked.

Grinning at him, Nancy answered, "I wouldn't miss it for anything."

"This is amazing," George whispered to Nancy and Mick later that night.

"I've never seen anything like it," Nancy agreed.

Ever since the corroboree had begun an hour earlier, Nancy's attention had been riveted to the aboriginal dancers and musicians. The site chosen for the ceremonial dance was on the outskirts of the Yungis' community. A fire blazed in an open area that was ringed with scrubby bushes, gum trees, and wattle trees. The corroboree was open to the public, and small groups of people were seated in the dark around the open circle where the Yungis performed. Nancy, George, and Mick were sitting on the ground near a thick clump of bushes, just beneath a canopy of twisted branches of a twenty-foot wattle. Frank, Joe, Harold, and Daphne were sitting with Gil and Clyde Branden, about halfway around the circle from them, and Dennis Moore sat near them. They all seemed to be awed.

The Yungi men were wearing loincloths that echoed the reds, yellows, and browns of the earth. They had tied white headbands around their foreheads and painted designs all over their skin with some kind of yellow pigment. A dozen men danced around the fire, while others created a rhythm by banging sticks and spears against the ground or tapping boomerangs together. The women, also dressed in earth tones, stood in the background, waving their arms and bodies rhythmically. The music was completely mesmerizing.

"What are those instruments?" George asked Mick. She pointed discreetly to some men who were seated cross-legged on the ground, blowing into hollow pieces of wood about four feet long.

"Those are didgeridoos," Mick told her. "It's a traditional aboriginal instrument. It produces only two notes, but the sound is unbelievable, isn't it?"

Nancy nodded. The music was soulful and unsettling, like the wind before a storm.

"Nellie told me that this dance tells the story of the Yungis' Dreaming," Mick went on. "The journey of the Honey Ant Father."

"Look. Isn't that Yami Whiteair?" George asked. She pointed to a dancer who was leading the others. His face was painted, but Nancy recognized his bushy mustache.

"Yes, it is. He's a powerful dancer, isn't he?"

Nancy turned toward a movement in the bushes to her right. What she saw was the glow from the fire reflecting on something metallic.

"Hey, that's a spear!" Nancy exclaimed. The sight of the spear's sharp tip had jolted Nancy from her dreamy state. "It's pointed over here!"

"Huh?" George swiveled her head around.

A lightning bolt of fear shot through Nancy. Before she could say another word, the spear shot out from the bushes, flying right toward her, George, and Mick!

Chapter

Eighteen

Frank's breath caught in his throat as he saw the spear fly out from the bushes, straight toward Nancy's group.

He started to yell, but his voice was overpowered by the Yungis' music. Frank watched in horror as Nancy, with the spear just inches from her head, twisted out of its path, pulling George and Mick with her. A split second later the spear hit the ground next to them.

"Joe, come on!" Frank grabbed his brother by the collar and pulled him to his feet.

"Hey! What's the big idea?"

"Someone just tried to kill Nancy!" Frank said, scouring the bushes with his eyes.

"What!" Joe whipped his head in Nancy's direction. "How—"

"Someone threw a spear at her from that brush over there," Frank said. He was already sprinting toward the bushes. The tangle of scrubby branches was surprisingly thick, and tall enough to hide someone. "Come on, before whoever threw it gets away."

"I'm right behind you," Joe called.

A quick glance told Frank that Nancy had pushed herself up and was running toward the bushes, too, a flashlight in her hand. The corroboree was so enthralling that no one else seemed to have noticed the spear. Frank focused all his attention on the shadowy scrub bushes. He hadn't gotten a look at whoever threw the spear, but he thought he saw a dark silhouette retreating farther into the bushes.

Nancy reached the edge of the scrub bushes half a step ahead of him. Together they plunged in, with Nancy shining her flashlight ahead of them. Branches stung Frank's face and caught at his clothes, making it hard to keep his eyes focused ahead. Even with the flashlight, he couldn't see the person. The pounding rhythms of the corroboree echoed all around them. When they emerged on the other side of the bushes moments later, they still hadn't caught up to the person who'd thrown the spear.

"See anyone?" Nancy asked, flicking her beam over the trees, bushes, and rocks surrounding the clearing.

Frank shook his head. "We can't check out every dark shadow where someone could be hiding." He turned around just as Mick and George pushed their way out of the bushes. Joe was still crashing around behind them. "He got away, huh?" George asked.

Nancy nodded. "It couldn't have been Yami Whiteair," she said. "He was dancing."

"The Royces aren't even here, but that doesn't mean they didn't sneak into the area to make the attack," Frank added.

"Well, whoever that was wasn't kidding around," Mick said soberly. "One of us could have been killed." He squeezed Nancy's hand, and Frank caught the intensity of feeling that shot between them.

"We only have one other suspect," Nancy said. "And that's—"

"You guys! Check this out," Joe interrupted, coming up to them. He was holding a small piece of fabric, which Nancy took from him.

"Looks like part of a denim shirt," she said. "Let's go back to the corroboree to see if we can find a shirt to match."

When they reached the edge of the clearing and could see the dancers and spectators again, George drew in her breath. "I knew it!" she said. "Guess who happens to be wearing a ripped denim shirt?"

"Clyde Branden," Frank said in a low voice. In the glow of the fire, he could see Branden's skin through the rip in his sleeve.

"Check out his face," Joe added. "Those scratches look pretty fresh—maybe he got them when he was running away from us through the bushes."

"I wish I knew what that guy was up to," Mick said darkly.

"We know someone promised him opals, and that some girl has caused a problem," Nancy said. "Mick and I overheard that much when we went to his office."

"But what you don't know for sure is whether Nellie is the girl," Frank said. "And if she is, we still have to figure out why she's a problem and what Branden plans on doing about it."

George nodded. "Plus we still don't know who promised Branden the opals to begin with."

Nancy stared at the dancers for a long moment, her brow furrowed in concentration. "I don't think it's a coincidence that Clyde Branden suddenly shows up in the same town the opals were stolen from. His vacation story is definitely bogus." Raising a brow at George and Mick, she added, "He said he's staying at the Flat Hill Lodge. I say we look through his things to see if we can find out what he has to do with the stolen opals and Nellie's disappearance."

"Sounds like a good idea," Frank agreed. "I wish Joe and I could help you out, but we've got plans to head out to Tracker Jordan's sheep station tomorrow. This time, if we're lucky, we might actually make it!"

"Thanks for waiting, guys," George said the next morning, hurrying into the restaurant at the lodge. She sat down at the table where Nancy and Mick were lingering over the remains of their breakfast. "Did Branden leave yet?"

Nancy shook her head. "We've been keeping an eye on the lobby, but so far he hasn't shown. Someone else is here, though." She gave a subtle nod across the restaurant, where Dennis Moore sat reading a paper. "Don't you guys think it's weird, the way Moore is hanging around Flat Hill but hasn't been at the scenes of any of the poachings?"

George shrugged, following Nancy's gaze. "If he's behind the poachings, maybe he's here to put pressure on the person who's doing his dirty work."

"Or to take any animals that the poacher bags for him," Mick added.

After finishing her pancakes and fresh kiwi, George had decided to stop at the Outback Adventures office to see how the wounded cockatoo was doing. Nancy was just beginning to wonder if something might be wrong, when George returned.

"Did you see the cockatoo?" Nancy asked. "Is it going to be okay?"

"I don't know," George answered, frowning. She waited while Regina Bourke refilled her coffee cup, then said, "It's hardly moving, and it won't eat. Daphne's pretty worried. She's afraid to move it."

"The poor creature," Nancy said. "I still can't believe someone would purposely harm—"

She broke off and stared through the restaurant's entrance. Clyde Branden had just appeared in the lobby, carrying a pack. "There he is," she said. "And we're in luck. Looks like he's ready to bush walk. That means he'll be gone awhile."

Just then a horn sounded outside, and Branden headed toward the entrance. "He's leaving," Mick said. He motioned to Regina for their bill, then checked with Nancy and George. "Ready?"

"You bet," Nancy told him.

When they'd gotten to the lodge that morning, Nancy had managed to get a peek at the registration book. She'd found out that Branden was staying in room seven. Now, as they left the restaurant, she was relieved to see that the lobby and registration desk were deserted. Motioning for Mick and George to follow, Nancy hurried up the wooden steps to a hallway with about a dozen doors on either side. Room seven was halfway down the hall to the left. Nancy had brought her lock-picking set with her. She went to work with a slender metal instrument. In a matter of seconds the lock popped open, and they hurried inside.

"Where do we start?" Nancy wondered aloud. The furniture looked as if it hadn't been changed in the last forty years. The bed had a scratched metal frame, and the mirror on the wall was flecked with imperfections. The faded blue brocade of an overstuffed armchair in one corner matched the fabric of the window curtains.

Mick nodded at the leather briefcase that lay on a wooden desk between the room's two windows. "Why would a man who's on vacation bring that along?"

"Good question," Nancy said. "I didn't even notice it yesterday. I guess we were too busy trying to keep our cover story straight."

While Mick strode across the room and flipped open the case, George went to one of the windows. "I'll be lookout."

"Good idea," Nancy agreed. She nodded to a suitcase on the floor next to the bed. It had been opened but not unpacked, and clothes filled its two sides. "I guess I'll start here."

Nancy was slipping her hand beneath a pile of shirts, when Mick murmured, "Nothing in here about opals, but there is something interesting—"

He was interrupted by George's low voice. "I wonder where *she's* going?"

"Who?" Nancy asked.

"Daphne. She told me she was going to be in the Outback Adventures office all morning," George explained. "Now she's getting in her Range Rover, and she's got the cockatoo with her."

"I thought she told you the bird was too sick to be moved," Mick said.

"That's what worries me," George admitted. "Do you think she lied to me?"

Nancy wasn't sure what to say. She knew that Daphne and George had gotten friendly over the last few days, but the young woman was acting suspiciously. "Maybe we'd better follow her," Nancy suggested.

"You mean, just leave here?" Mick asked, gesturing around Branden's room.

"I don't like dropping the search, either, but this could be important to the Hardys' case, and Frank and Joe aren't here to follow up," Nancy said. "They're out at Tracker Jordan's station."

"Frank and Joe helped me out a lot while you two were gone," George added. "If Branden's on a bush walk, he'll be gone for hours. We should have time to finish searching later."

Nancy started for the door. "We'd better hurry if we don't want to lose her. Let's go!"

"Joe and I appreciate your giving us some pointers on bush walking and camping in the outback," Frank said to Tracker Jordan.

Joe groaned inwardly and shifted from foot to foot on the hard, trampled-down earth outside one of Jordan's sheep pens. He and Frank had found the rancher with some of his workers in the penned-in area. Playing up to Tracker this way was torture. Joe and Frank had agreed that it might be the only way to get the opportunity to search the station for evidence linking Jordan to the poaching.

"Yeah," Joe said, swallowing his pride. "We're going to spend a week roughing it on our own before we head back to the States. We just want to make sure we don't do anything dumb."

Tracker gave them a strange look, but all he said was, "Sure. I'll be with you in a sec."

While Tracker finished instructing his workers, Joe took in the station's two-story house, which was across a packed-dirt yard from the sheep pen and other outbuildings. Fences stretched north and west as far as Joe could see, and sheep grazed on the scrubby land.

"I'm just wondering . . ." Tracker's voice made Joe turn back to the sheep pen. Tracker was just closing the pen's wooden gate behind him." Since when did I become your biggest hero?"

Frank shot Joe an uneasy glance, then said, "I guess you could say that Joe and I have learned the hard way that you know your way around the outback."

"I hope you'll remember that from now on, mates," Tracker said with an arrogant smirk. It took a lot of self-control for Joe to keep from telling the guy what he really thought. He clamped his mouth shut while Tracker led them through a side door and into the kitchen.

"So, what do you want to know?" Tracker asked.

"We've done a lot of camping," Joe said as he and Frank sat at the table opposite Tracker. "But out here—do we need any special equipment? Like maybe some kind of gun for protection?"

He was hoping to get Tracker to show them his guns, but the rancher just gave him and Frank a long, hard look. "Not necessarily," Tracker finally answered. "The biggest danger is from fire. If you get caught in one, no gun will help you."

Joe heard the sound of an approaching vehicle. Tracker stood up to peer out the window. Then he turned back to Frank and Joe. "Be right back," he told them, heading for the kitchen door.

As soon as he disappeared outside, Frank and Joe jumped to their feet to look out the window. Daphne was just pulling to a stop in the yard.

"What's *she* doing here?" Frank whispered. "And why does she have the cockatoo with her?"

"We can find out soon enough," Joe answered.

He jumped up and glanced around. "Let's check for a custom-made rifle while we have the chance." Through an open doorway, he saw a couch and some chairs. He was about to head toward them, when Frank stopped him.

"Joe, look!" Frank was pointing out the window, a tight expression on his face.

Daphne had placed the cockatoo on a weathered picnic table at the edge of the yard, and Tracker Jordan was moving purposefully toward his truck. Joe tensed when he saw Tracker reach toward his gun rack.

"Hey!" Joe froze as he realized what was happening. "He's going to shoot the cockatoo!"

Chapter

Nineteen

"Oh, MY GOSH!" George said. She leaned over the dashboard and stared through the dusty windshield. "It's Tracker—and he's got a rifle!"

Nancy was sitting between George and Mick, staring through binoculars. They had stopped at the end of the dusty drive leading to Tracker's station just as Daphne pulled up next to the house. "He's aiming it at the cockatoo, and Daphne's just standing there! Mick, we have to stop him!"

Mick had already thrown the truck into gear. He floored the gas pedal, and the truck flew forward so suddenly that Nancy jolted backward against the seat. Tracker and Daphne were bound to see them, but they couldn't worry about hiding if they wanted to save the wounded cockatoo.

"I could have sworn that Daphne really cared

about that bird," George said. "Why would she bring it out here for Tracker to kill?"

Nancy could hear the distress in George's voice, but she kept her attention focused on Tracker. The truck was bouncing so much that she couldn't use the binoculars, but she could still see him. For a brief second, he lowered the gun and glanced in their direction. Then he aimed it at the bird again.

"Hurry!" Nancy urged. She knew Mick was driving as fast as he could, but they were still a hundred feet away. There was no way they could get there before—

"No!" Nancy heard George's cry at the same moment she saw Tracker fire the rifle. Seconds later Mick zoomed up next to Daphne's Range Rover and screeched to a halt. As Nancy dove out the passenger door behind George, she saw Frank and Joe confronting Tracker.

"You two are in trouble now," Frank said.

"Major trouble," Joe added.

Tracker lowered the rifle to his side. He and Daphne both gaped at the five teenagers converging on them. "What's going on here?" Tracker demanded.

Ignoring him, George went over to Daphne. "I can't believe I thought you were a friend," she said, her cheeks flushed with anger. "I thought you cared about the cockatoo. How could you bring it here to let him shoot it?"

Daphne seemed genuinely confused. "What are you talking about?"

Before George could answer, Tracker let out a

deep, booming laugh. "This is rich. You *detectives* are way off the mark this time. Take a look at your *dead* bird."

Nancy couldn't believe how callous he was being. She hadn't been able to bring herself to look at the cockatoo. Now she turned toward the weathered table. She could hardly believe her eyes.

"It's still alive!" Mick said under his breath. He sounded just as surprised as Nancy felt.

Nancy and George rushed over to the bird, which was still wrapped in Frank's shirt. The cockatoo was perfectly still, but its tiny black eyes were alert. While George scooped it up and held it protectively, Nancy looked over her shoulder at Tracker.

"If you didn't shoot the bird, then what . . . ?" Just then she caught sight of a dead snake lying in the dust a few yards from the cockatoo. Its head had been shot clean off.

"Tiger snake," Tracker said tersely. "They're deadly, in case you didn't know."

"This doesn't change the fact that you two have been acting very suspiciously," Frank told Tracker and Daphne. "Don't think for a second that Joe and I are going to back off this case. If you two are poaching, we'll catch you eventually."

"What Daphne and I do is none of your business!" Tracker burst out angrily.

"Tracker, please. Let's just tell them, so they'll stop bothering us." Daphne gently placed a hand on his arm, which surprised Frank. Tracker hesitated, then nodded.

"Tracker and I aren't poaching," Daphne explained. "We're dating."

Joe's mouth fell open. "Dating?" he echoed. "Then why the cloak-and-dagger routine? Are you trying to tell us that when you ran Frank, Harold, and me into that swamp, you were on a date?"

"We know it was your knife we found near the night glider," Frank added. He crossed his arms over his chest and fixed Daphne with a probing stare. "How do you explain that? And why wouldn't you tell me what you and Dennis Moore were talking about?"

"How could you go out with someone who kills the wildlife around here?" George asked Daphne. "Gil told us Tracker's been fined for shooting kangaroos."

Tracker opened his mouth, but before he could speak, Daphne said, "He's not like that anymore." Her cheeks reddened as she glanced at the group surrounding her. "Look, I admit that Tracker used to be a little—reckless about killing wallabies."

"Used to be?" Joe repeated doubtfully.

"Yes," Daphne insisted. "I know what you're thinking—I used to feel the same way. That's why we kept our relationship a secret. Tracker has such a terrible reputation that I wasn't ready to go public yet." She gave Tracker an apologetic glance. "I guess I was a little embarrassed."

"So that's why you've been lying about spending time in the office," George said. "You didn't want us to know you were meeting Tracker."

Daphne nodded. "I know it wasn't fair of us to strand you in that swamp," she told Frank and Joe, "but you were so sure we were the poachers, we couldn't resist teaching you a lesson. Then, once the rain started, I got stuck in the mud myself. By the time Tracker and I got my Rover moving again, we knew we'd never be able to make it back to help you. We were lucky to get back to town ourselves."

"You're saying that Tracker came back to the swamp yesterday specifically to help us, not to poach the cockatoo?" Joe asked dubiously.

"You don't have to believe us, but it's the truth," Tracker said.

Frank's gut instinct told him that Tracker and Daphne were telling the truth, but they still hadn't answered some important questions. "What was your knife doing near that glider, Daphne?"

"And why did you bring the cockatoo here?" Nancy added.

"Second question first," Daphne said. She took the bird from George and carefully handed it over to Tracker. "Tracker is quite skilled in healing animals. That was one of the things I learned once when I was stuck with two flat tires and Tracker helped me out. We found a parrot with a wounded wing, and Tracker brought it here to care for it until it was well enough to return to the bush."

"We started spending more time together after that, and the rest is history," Tracker added. Frank was impressed by the gentle way Tracker handled the bird as he unwound the gauze Daphne had used to bandage the wing. After examining the wing,

Tracker left the cockatoo on the table, went to one of the outbuildings across the yard, and disappeared inside.

"I admit he used to kill wallabies and dingoes—those are Australia's wild dogs. But since we've been seeing each other, he's reformed," Daphne insisted. "The only reason he killed that red kangaroo the other day is because it was caught up in his fence."

"The knife?" Joe pressed.

Daphne's eyes strayed to the outbuilding Tracker had gone into. "After I left our campsite that night, I heard someone in the brush. I didn't find anyone, but the sudden rifle shot made me drop my knife," she explained. She watched as Tracker came back through the door with a first-aid box and returned to the table. "After that, everything happened so fast—I didn't have time to look for it."

"And when Joe found it, you thought you'd look guilty if we knew it was yours," Mick guessed.

"You've got the picture," Daphne told him. "As for Dennis Moore, when he stopped by the office, all he did was ask me for a brochure. Said something about coming back to hike in the Comet Creek gorges sometime in the future."

"If it was that innocent, then why didn't you just tell me when I asked about him?" Frank asked.

Daphne flashed him a moody glance before answering. "It really irked me that you two were so willing to think I was a poacher. I figured I didn't owe you any explanations—about Tracker, about Dennis Moore, about anything."

"I guess I did come down a little hard on you," Joe admitted.

Frank shook his head in amazement. "You know, Gil told Joe and me how you hate each other. Boy, is he going to be surprised when he hears you're dating."

"I had the same thought myself when I saw his plane touch down out here Tuesday evening," Tracker said. He had spread some kind of salve on the bird's wing and was now wrapping the wing with fresh gauze.

"That was the same day we spotted Nellie in Airlie Beach," Nancy said. "He must have been on his way back." She frowned. "But Flat Hill's landing strip is to the east. Why would he land way over here to the west?"

"I'm surprised he'd do that, with his fuel line giving him so many problems," Daphne added, frowning. "Landing in the outback is rougher on a plane than using a landing strip."

Tracker shrugged. "No doubt Gil had his reasons, but I don't generally butt into another man's business. I was busy fixing a fence at my eastern border at the time—didn't pay much mind to what he was about. All I know is that he touched down near a huge baobab tree out there. I was just starting to wonder if he was having trouble with his plane, when he took off again."

"That's funny. He never mentioned anything about it to Joe or me," Frank put in. "I wonder if—"

"I almost forgot!" Mick exclaimed, snapping his

fingers. "When we were in Clyde Branden's room, I saw something very interesting in his briefcase."

"That's right," George said. "You mentioned something just before we left to come here. I was so worried about the cockatoo that I totally forgot."

"Branden had some papers," Mick went on excitedly. "Records of a fifty-thousand-dollar loan he made—that's a little less than forty thousand U.S. dollars. Guess who the money went to?"

"Gil Strickland?" Joe supplied.

Nancy was instantly alert. "Didn't he say he took out a loan to keep Outback Adventures alive?" she asked. "What if the only way he could pay back the loan was by stealing the Royces' black opals?"

"Nellie must have stumbled onto him," Mick added. "No wonder she ran from us at Shute Harbour. She must have panicked when she saw Gil with us."

"Wait a second," Frank said, holding up a hand. "Gil is an old friend of our dad. I can't believe that—I mean, I just don't think—"

"That he's a criminal?" Daphne frowned. "I can't see it, either. I've worked with Gil for two years, and I've never known him to break the law." She let out a sigh before adding, "He has been distracted lately, though."

"Money troubles will do that to a bloke," Tracker said, without looking up from the wounded cockatoo. He had finished bandaging the bird's wing and was giving it some water with an eye dropper.

"We can't convict the guy without some proof," Joe put in.

Mick was already jogging toward Nellie's truck. "Well then, let's go get some."

"Nellie's life could be at stake," Nancy added. "Do you guys mind if we search Gil's house?"

Frank looked at Joe, who shrugged. "I guess not," Joe said.

"Good luck," Daphne told them. "Let us know what happens."

During the drive to Gil's house, Frank kept thinking of the man. He had a hard time seeing Gil as a criminal.

"Maybe it wasn't him," Joe said.

Frank shifted his gaze from the road long enough to see that his brother was staring at him. "I don't know. Gil does talk about money problems a lot. And he said something about his troubles being over soon, remember? It doesn't look good."

They were both quiet for the rest of the trip. When they pulled up at Gil's house later, Mick, Nancy, and George were right behind them in Nellie's truck.

"Okay, here's the living room and kitchen," Frank said when they got inside. "Plus Gil's room down that hall and a storage shed out back. I think we can rule out the guest room. Joe and I would have noticed anything suspicious in there."

"We're looking for black opals or liquid nitrogen —that's what was used to break into the Royces' safe. Or for anything showing that Gil knows what happened to Nellie," Nancy said. "George and I'll start in the shed."

"I'll show you where," Joe offered. While he led

Nancy and George to the back door, off the kitchen area, Mick went to the couch and bent to look underneath it. Frank headed for Gil's bedroom. If Gil wanted to hide something where he and Joe wouldn't find it, that seemed the most likely spot.

"Bed . . . desk . . . closet . . ." Frank murmured. It felt weird to be treating Gil's room like a crime scene, but he had to start somewhere. He went over to the bed and slid a hand beneath the mattress. Might as well check the easy spots before going through all the things in Gil's desk and closet.

"Hmm. What's this?" Frank's hand rubbed against a soft piece of fabric underneath the mattress. It probably wasn't anything, but to be sure, he pulled it out.

He stared in dismay at the blue felt bag in his hand. The letters *RM* were printed on the felt in gold letters, and Frank had a sinking suspicion that he knew what the letters stood for: Royce Mining.

Chapter

Twenty

Y OU GUYS, look what I found!"

At the sound of his brother's voice, Joe looked up from the bookcase he was searching. Frank came into the living room from the hallway, anything but happy. "What is it?" Joe asked.

"I didn't see any opals, but isn't this the kind of bag gems are stored in?" Frank said. "I found it under Gil's mattress."

Joe let out a low whistle when he saw the blue felt bag Frank held out. *"RM,"* he said grimly. "If that means what I think it means, this is bad news."

Mick straightened up from the couch and strode over to Frank. "So Gil *did* steal the opals. He must have handed over the stones to Clyde Branden already—or hidden them somewhere else. Did you see anything to show that Gil knows what happened to Nellie?"

"Sorry," Frank answered.

Just then the Hardys heard the back door bang open. A moment later George and Nancy walked into the living room. "You guys," Joe said, "it looks as if Frank found the bag the black opals were in when they were stolen."

"Nancy and I hit the jackpot, too." George said. "Gil is definitely the opal thief. We found a container of liquid nitrogen in the shed. And this."

Joe gaped at the rectangular piece of bark she held up. "The bark carving!" he exclaimed. "Gil was with us when you opened it. He said he was flying to the coast, but—"

"He must have stolen the carving from Yami Whiteair before he left, so that no one would be able to decipher it," Nancy finished.

"Mind if I have a look?" Mick asked, going over to George. "Nellie taught me some about the symbols she uses." George handed over the carving, and Mick sat on the couch and looked at it closely. "This is almost exactly like the drawing Yami made for us, Nancy."

Joe and George leaned over the couch back, while Nancy and Frank sat next to Mick. "According to Nellie's grandfather, that grid of circles represents the town of Flat Hill," Mick said.

Nancy pointed to two symbols next to the grid. "Do you know what those mean? That one looks like a kangaroo, doesn't it?"

"Yes. And I'm pretty sure the dots of that other symbol represent fire," Mick said. "The dots are in a circle, though. I don't know what that means."

"Hey! Couldn't it be an opal?" Frank said suddenly. "The colors in the one Paul Kidder had looked exactly like sparks of flame."

"I bet you're right," Nancy said, sitting forward excitedly. "And I just thought of something else—the logo for Outback Adventures is a kangaroo, and these two symbols are at the edge of town—"

"At the exact same spot where the Royces' office is," George finished. "So Nellie was trying to tell us that Gil is the opal thief."

"Looks that way," Mick answered. "Gil must have realized that she was onto him, and he threatened her or tried to kill her. That's why she ran."

Joe saw the frown on Nancy's face. "Actually, she might not be hiding anymore," she said. She held up a crumpled rag she'd been clutching in her hand. Joe took one whiff, and his nostrils immediately started to itch from the chemical odor.

"That's chloroform."

Nancy nodded soberly. "When Mick and I were following Nellie on Thomas Island, I smelled a funny odor. There were so many fragrant flowers around, I didn't realize what it was—until just now."

"That was right before we found the taipan in your pack," Mick said.

"Gil must have gotten to the island somehow and followed *us* while we were following Nellie. I bet he planted the taipan to distract us so he could get to Nellie before we did," Nancy went on. "He had to shut her up before she could tell us what she'd seen."

"So he knocked her out with chloroform?" George said. "I still don't understand how he managed it."

"I bet he made up that whole story about picking up clients," Frank said grimly. "He probably planned to go after Nellie from the start."

Nancy glanced worriedly around at everyone else. "I haven't figured out the details yet, but I bet anything that when Gil landed out near Tracker's station, he had Nellie with him," she said. "That's why he touched down in such an out-of-the-way place—so no one else would know. We're just lucky that Tracker happened to spot the plane."

George drew in her breath, giving Nancy a horrified look. "Do you think he—killed her?"

"He couldn't have," Mick said firmly.

Joe wasn't so sure. He said, "There's only one way to find out."

Nancy kept her eyes glued to the horizon as Frank drove the Range Rover north along the eastern boundary of Tracker Jordan's station. Mick and George sat silently beside her. The Hardys hadn't said much either. Nancy could tell they were thinking about what they might find when they got to the baobab tree Tracker had told them about.

The wind had picked up, and somehow the stiff

breeze helped Nancy to think. "We have to be careful," she said, breaking the silence. "Clyde Branden and Gil could be out there, too. They know we're investigating, so we should be prepared for trouble."

"I'm glad we called the police," Frank added.

"They might not be here for an hour or so, though," George pointed out. "It took Officer Downs a while to show up after the opal theft, remember?"

Suddenly Mick grabbed Nancy's arm. "Look at that tree. It must be the one Tracker was talking about!" he exclaimed.

The tree Mick was pointing to was about half a mile away. It was twice as big as any others they'd seen, and it had a round, bulbous trunk that was almost as wide around as its cap of branches. As Frank headed for the tree, Nancy felt her body tense. The baobab's trunk was at least ten feet across, its branches gnarled and without leaves.

"Amazing," George breathed. "It looks as if it's been there forever."

"I don't see Gil's Range Rover," Frank commented. "We're in luck."

Nancy hoped so. They were about a hundred yards from the baobab tree when Joe said, "Is it my imagination, or is there an opening at the base of the trunk?"

Peering ahead, Nancy saw that he was right. "It looks as if the tree might be hollow," she said.

"Please let her be there," Mick said under his

breath. "Please let her be all right." When they got to the tree, he barely waited for Frank to come to a stop before jumping out of the Rover.

As soon as Frank turned off the engine, Nancy heard a melodic sound coming from the tree. "Is that singing?" she asked.

"Nellie!" Mick sprinted to the hole at the base of the tree, which was a few feet wide and came to a ragged point about three feet from the ground. Nancy was half a step behind him when he reached the opening, braced his hands on the smooth bark, and bent to look inside the opening.

"It *is* her!" Nancy exclaimed.

The inside of the baobab tree was completely hollow and about eight feet across. Nellie was sitting on the ground near the opening, her wrists and ankles bound. She was wearing the same yellow scarf she'd had on at the Great Barrier Reef, but it was now dirty.

"Where've you been, Mick?" Nellie asked, grinning. Nancy couldn't believe how calm she looked.

Mick practically dove inside the tree and started to untie Nellie. "You're all right! I can't believe we finally found you!"

Nancy, George, Frank, and Joe all squeezed into the baobab tree behind him. About four feet from the ground the trunk narrowed, so they had to squat shoulder to shoulder around Nellie. For the next few minutes, everyone talked at once, introducing Frank and Joe and telling Nellie how they'd found her.

"We haven't found the opals yet," Mick said as he finished untying Nellie, "but the most important thing is that you're all right."

"No thanks to Gil Strickland," Nellie said, rubbing her ankles where they'd been bound. "I went to the Royces' office early Monday to leave Ian and Marian a note asking them to meet with our lawyer. When I saw a light, I decided to speak with them in person."

"Only it wasn't them?" Joe guessed.

Nellie nodded. "Gil was about to leave with the opals. When he saw me, at first he tried to buy me off. He gave me a story about being blackmailed into the theft by someone he owed money to," she went on.

"Clyde Branden," Frank supplied. "We're pretty sure that part of his story is true, actually."

"Gil went berserk when I refused to accept his payoff," Nellie said. "Said he'd pin the theft on me, and then he jumped me. Threw me against a wall of photos—that's how I got this," she said, pointing to the dirty bandage on her arm. "We made quite a mess. I was lucky to get away at all."

George was squatting with her arms wrapped around her knees. "Why didn't you go to the police?"

Nellie rolled her eyes. "I knew it would be my word against Gil's. Who do you think the police would believe, an Aborigine who's been fighting with the mine owners, or a man who's been a respectable guide in Flat Hill for years?" She shook her head in disgust. "I would have been arrested right away."

"But Nancy, George, and I were coming back from Comet Creek that same day," Mick put in. "We could have put together enough evidence to back up your story—like the liquid nitrogen Gil used to break into the Royces' safe, and the felt bag the opals were in."

"I wasn't sure when you'd be back, and I didn't think I could wait and take the chance of getting caught," Nellie explained. "I didn't want to leave a message in my handwriting—it might have been used against me. I managed to make the bark carving for you, Mick, and leave it at the post office, but I wasn't sure you'd even get it." A pained expression came over Nellie's face, as if she were reliving the awful hours right after her run-in with Gil. "I didn't want to get Granddad involved, either. I thought the police might call him an accessory to the theft if they knew he'd seen me. All I wanted to do was get out of Flat Hill fast. I wasn't even thinking about where to go, but I knew Roger made his supply runs early in the morning."

"What made you go to Clyde Branden's office?" Joe asked. "That guy seems to be nothing but trouble."

"I know that now," Nellie said ruefully. "It wasn't until I was on the supply plane with Roger that I remembered that Gil had mentioned Clyde Branden's name and that he was in Airlie Beach. Gil was in such a rage, I don't think he realized he made the slip. I thought if I could track down Branden, maybe I could find a way to search for something to prove that Gil and Clyde Branden were the thieves, not me. But by the time I got to his office on Monday evening, it was already closed."

"So you went back Tuesday morning, when we saw you," Nancy put in.

"Yes. Before I went, I bought a ticket to Thomas Island—I knew I might need to lie low for a while, and I have a friend who works there." Nellie shook her head. "Branden was quite suspicious when I stopped in at his office. Even though I didn't tell him my name, I'm sure he guessed. Gil must have called and told him about—"

Nellie broke off talking. She turned her head toward the opening in the baobab tree and sniffed.

"Fire."

The one word sent a shiver through Nancy. She had heard about Australian bush fires that raged out of control for weeks. Now that Nellie mentioned it, she caught a whiff of the vague, smoky scent, too.

"This could be bad," Frank said, breaking the uneasy silence that had fallen over the group. He bolted toward the hole in the tree trunk. Everyone else scrambled behind him.

"Oh, no!" George breathed, once they were all outside. "Look!"

Facing into the wind, Nancy scanned the southern horizon. The first thing she saw was smoke rising from the ground. Then she saw the flames spreading across the horizon in a long line.

"Hey!" she said. She did a double take as she spotted a flash of blue at one end of the fire, near a clump of gum trees. "That's the Outback Adventures Rover!" she cried. As she watched, the Rover started south, while the flames pushed north.

"That must be Gil and Clyde Branden," Joe said. "They set this fire on purpose—and it's heading this way!"

"To get rid of us," Nellie added.

"But that's crazy!" Mick exclaimed. "That fire will kill every living thing in its path. It could ruin hundreds of acres of outback."

While he spoke, Nancy kept her eyes on the fire, and she didn't like what she saw. Flames leapt to consume a gum tree, then kept racing toward them at amazing speed. The sky was already filling with smoke—the flames crackled more and more loudly every second.

"You guys, the wind is building. It's blowing the fire out of control!" Nancy cried. "In a few minutes those flames will be right on top of us!"

Chapter

Twenty-One

We're sunk!" Joe cried. He felt his stomach bottom out as he stared at the raging bush fire.

"Everyone into the Rover," Nellie said urgently. "We have to drive around the fire. It's our only hope."

Frank, Nancy, George, Mick, and Nellie made running dives for the vehicle. Joe leapt behind the wheel, turned the key, and floored the gas. "We *have* to make it," George said. She and Frank were in the front passenger seat, while Mick, Nancy, and Nellie had squeezed into the back.

"Come on," Joe urged under his breath, driving faster.

"Watch out!" Nancy yelled from the backseat.

Joe swerved sharply to the left to avoid hitting a large kangaroo that was in their path. The Range

Rover tipped precariously on two wheels before righting itself. Joe had been so intent on the fire that he hadn't even seen the animal.

"There are hundreds of them!" George cried.

Kangaroos, emus, and dozens of other animals were fleeing as fast as they could. Above them, birds dotted the smoke-filled sky. Their cries mixed with the loud roar of the spreading blaze. "This is unreal!" Frank exclaimed.

The fire was racing north, toward them, and spreading east at the same time. Joe headed southeast, toward the edge of the wall of flames. He had to keep slowing down to avoid animals, rocks, and trees. The fire was fast outpacing them. "I don't think we can make it!"

He broke into a cough. Hot smoke seared his throat and stung his eyes, and sweat poured down his face, arms, and legs. Glancing in the rearview mirror, he saw that the others were burying their faces in their hands to keep from inhaling the smoke.

"We'll have to turn around and head downwind," Frank yelled. "It's our only chance!"

Joe was about to pull into a U-turn, but Nellie said, "No! There's a creek over there, to the east. It will slow the flames. If we can cross to the other side before the flames jump the creek, there's a chance we can get around the fire."

Joe wasn't so sure, but he didn't dare let up on the accelerator for even a second. Any delay could mean the difference between life and death. The flames were only about a quarter mile away, and they were spreading north and east faster every second. "Any objections?" he called out.

No one answered. Even without looking, Joe could feel the others gauging their chances. The outback had turned into a nightmare of smoke and flames.

Except this was no nightmare.

The flames were only a few hundred yards in front of them when Mick pointed to the eastern edge of the blaze. "Look, it's slowing!" he yelled above the deafening roar of the fire.

Joe spotted a small rivulet a few hundred feet away. "The creek," Nellie said.

"It doesn't look very big," George said worriedly. "The fire will jump it in no time."

Joe had to agree. As he drove toward the stream, he saw that it was only eight or ten feet across. Flames were already licking over the water's surface, just a dozen feet from them now. He was so focused on the fire that he could hardly believe it when he heard Nellie start to sing—a high, melodic tune that hung in the air.

"What are you doing?" Nancy asked anxiously.

"Singing up the stream," Nellie answered. "Bring the water up higher to help us."

Joe didn't have time to question her. "Hold on to your hats, everyone. Here we go!"

They bounced down a small embankment, then jolted into the brown water. Joe was thrown forward against the steering wheel, but he made himself keep his foot on the gas. "It's only a few feet deep," he called to the others. "If we're lucky, we can—"

"Look out!" George screamed. A second later a flaming branch on the surface of the water hit the side of the Rover, sending sparks flying over them before it bounced off and floated downstream. Joe eased forward while the others batted at the sparks. The fire was so close now, he felt as if his eyebrows would be singed right off his face. All of them were coughing from the acrid black smoke.

"Oh, no! It's jumping the stream!" Frank yelled.

Joe felt a sinking sensation in the pit of his stomach when he saw that airborne sparks had already lit the dry grass and scrub on the other side of the creek. In a matter of seconds the flames were raging several feet high.

"Faster," Nellie urged. "We've got to get around it—now!"

Joe gunned the engine, and the wheels kicked up mud and water. For one awful second he didn't think the wheels would catch, then all at once they bounced onto the far bank. Gritting his teeth, he sped up the embankment. The fire was even with them now. It was picking up speed.

"Joe! What?"

George's exclamation was cut short as Joe yanked the wheel to the right, racing right into the fire's path. It was a desperate move, but it was their only hope. "Duck down, everyone!" he yelled.

He scrunched down low behind the steering wheel. A moment later fire was all around them.

Joe felt as if the steering wheel would melt. He closed his eyes for just a second, and when he reopened them . . .

"Hey! We did it!"

The flames were behind them now, moving downwind away from them. Joe immediately slowed to a stop and glanced around to make sure there weren't any flames on them or the Range Rover. Nancy, Mick, Nellie, George, and Frank were all coughing.

"We're . . . actually . . . alive," George said between coughs. Her face was stained with soot and sweat. "Good going, Hardy."

Joe shivered when he glanced behind them at the blaze that was roaring northward. "Thanks, Nellie. If you hadn't told us about this creek, we would still be trying to outrun that sucker."

"And I doubt we would have succeeded," Frank added, staring grimly at the bush fire. "How could Gil do something like this?"

The mention of Gil's name jolted Joe into action again. "We can't just let him and Clyde Branden get away. They'll probably try to leave in Gil's plane." He leaned forward and threw the vehicle into gear again. "I'm heading for the airstrip."

"There!" Frank said, pointing. "Isn't that Gil's plane?"

Nancy leaned forward from the backseat and squinted. They had just driven past Flat Hill and were approaching the air strip. Nancy saw the small propeller plane at one end of the strip. A man was leaning over the plane's engine, and another was lifting bags from the blue Range Rover nearby. "Gil and Clyde Branden are both there," she said.

"Hurry, before they take off!" Mick urged.

They were still several hundred yards away when Nancy saw Gil snap to attention. He turned their way, then quickly closed the metal panel over the engine.

"They've spotted us," George said.

Nancy felt every muscle in her body tense up as she watched Gil run to the cockpit and jump in. Seconds later Clyde Branden climbed in the other side. It was a race against time. Please, *please* don't let Gil and Branden win, she prayed silently.

"We've got you suckers," Joe said under his breath as he drove onto the runway.

Only a hundred feet to go, Nancy thought. Seconds later she heard the plane's engine sputter. The propeller jerked in a slow circle, then spun to top speed as the engine roared to life.

Just as Gil started to inch the plane forward, Joe made a screeching stop right in front of the plane. Nancy saw the burning hatred on Gil Strickland's face as she, the Hardys, George, Mick, and Nellie all jumped out and raced for the plane. He must have realized he couldn't taxi around the Rover because he stopped the plane, popped open the cockpit door, and jumped to the runway.

Before he could run more than a few steps, Frank, Mick, and George were on top of him. Gil threw a punch at Mick, but Mick sidestepped the blow. A second later Frank caught Gil's hand and twisted it behind his back, while Mick and George helped restrain him. In a flash Nancy and Joe ran to the other side of the plane.

"Hold it, Branden!" Joe ordered.

Clyde Branden was already halfway out of the cockpit. Nancy tensed, ready to grab him if he tried to run. "Don't even think about it," she told him.

Branden's beady eyes flicked back and forth between Nancy and Joe. Nancy thought he might bolt, but after a long moment, he held up his hands. "All right. I'm coming down quietly. Anyhow, Strickland's the one you want, not me."

Gil glared at Clyde Branden and tried to jerk free from Mick's and Joe's grasp. "Why you—"

"You can forget the righteous act," Frank cut in. "Nellie told us everything."

As Nancy and Joe escorted Clyde Branden over to the others, Frank unzipped Gil's belt pack and fished out a bulging plastic bag filled with black opals.

"Frank already found the felt bag from Royce Mining that those were in," Nancy told Gil. "Did you think we wouldn't know where the opals came from, just because you removed them from the bag with the mine's initials on it?"

Gil glared at her but said nothing.

George let out a low whistle as she came over with a rope she'd gotten from the back of the Hardys' Range Rover. She and Mick tied Gil's hands behind his back while Nancy and Joe tied Clyde Branden's.

"The way we see it, Clyde Branden was putting pressure on you to get the opals," Nancy told Gil. Seeing his surprised look, she explained, "We know that he lent you fifty thousand dollars."

"Keep your mouth shut, Strickland!" Branden spat out, his face red with fury.

"If I'm going down, you're going down with me," Gil shot back. He stared moodily at the faces surrounding him. "The loan came due last month, but I didn't have the money to repay it, so Branden gave me an ultimatum. Either I steal the opals, or he was going to send some goons my way to make sure I paid the loan in flesh and blood."

Gil let out a sigh. "He's my ex-wife's brother. When I needed money to keep Outback Adventures going, I couldn't think of anyone else to turn to."

"The Royces told us that the stolen opals were worth over a hundred and fifty thousand. That's three times what you owe Clyde Branden," Mick pointed out.

"Which leaves enough money to keep me comfortable for a good while to come," Gil said. He must have seen the disgust on everyone's faces because he added bitterly, "You kids have no right to be so righteous. You don't know what it's like to struggle for a living, barely getting by year after year. And then Ian and Marian Royce waltz into town, and in no time they're rolling in money."

"That doesn't mean it's all right to steal from

them and then try to kill someone just because she caught you in the act," Mick said. "Not to mention trying to kill Nancy and me with that taipan."

"I wasn't about to let Nellie get away a second time!" Gil burst out angrily.

Nancy couldn't believe how twisted Gil's priorities had gotten. "You must have taken a private boat to Thomas Island, just as Mick and I did. Only you didn't land at the main dock," she guessed.

Gil glared at her before answering. "I waited until you two were gone, then arranged for a boat myself. When I got to Thomas Island, I docked at a cove just out of sight of the main beach, then hid in the trees behind you. You two never even knew I was there. After Nellie's boat docked, I followed all of you. Luckily, I had the foresight to borrow a taipan someone had caught in a plastic jar by the campsite."

"That was you we heard in the woods, not a wild animal," Mick said. "And when we went to investigate, you planted the taipan in Nancy's pack."

"Good guess," Gil told him. "I would have preferred not to kill you, but my future was at stake. The snake attack gave me enough time to run ahead to the clearing where Nellie was and knock her out with some chloroform I'd brought along."

"Why didn't you kill me right away?" Nellie asked, eyeing Gil calmly.

Gil avoided looking at Nellie as he answered. "I could see that your friends weren't going to back off their investigation until they found out exactly what had happened to you and why. But when I called Branden for help, he made it clear that I was on my own. That's why I held back his share of the opals. I knew Nellie could finger him."

"So you decided to keep her alive to use as leverage to convince Branden to help you deal with all of us," Mick said, shaking his head in disgust. "Gee, Gil, you're a real humanitarian."

"I figured no one would find her in that baobab tree," Gil went on, ignoring the comment. "But when I called Branden, he still wouldn't help me out."

Nancy couldn't believe Gil could look outraged, after all the awful things he had done. "I think Mick and I overheard Branden talking to you when we went to his office," she said, recalling the developer's comments about "the girl" and black opals. She glanced at him, but Branden remained silent.

"It wasn't until after your visit to Branden Developers," Gil said, nodding at Nancy and Mick, "that Clyde realized the problem wasn't going to go away easily. That's when he called and said he'd come and help me get rid of all you troublemakers."

"That must be the conversation *we* overheard, Joe," Frank put in. "Right before Gil flew back to Airlie Beach to pick up his so-called client."

Gil nodded. "We thought we could lure you into some kind of accident in the outback."

Branden let out a bitter laugh, breaking his long silence. "Happens all the time," he said. "Bush walkers get lost and are devoured by some wild beast. Quite often their bodies are never found." Nancy shivered at his cold, calculating tone.

"But when we saw your Rover," Gil said, "Clyde came up with the idea of the bush fire."

"That fire is probably still burning out of control," Frank said. "You two are responsible for totally ruining the outback north of here."

Nancy noticed that Gil at least had the decency to look uncomfortable. "Clyde figured the fire would get rid of all our problems at once. They're common enough that no one would think to suspect us."

"Well, there's one thing you didn't figure on," Joe put in. He put one arm around Nancy's shoulder and the other around Frank's. "Us."

"Mmm. I don't think I've ever had a barbie that tastes as good as this one," Nellie said that night.

Frank smiled across the table at her. "After two days of not eating, I'm not surprised to hear that. That's your third plateful of barbecued beef."

"Her grandfather, Yami, and some of the other Yungis have even more food waiting for her when she gets back home later," Mick added.

It had taken over an hour for Lou Downs and two other officers to make the trip to Flat Hill from their base in the larger town of Roma, to the south, but Gil Strickland and Clyde Branden were now safely in custody. Frank had been relieved when Officer Downs told them that the bush fire was under control, thanks to fire fighters who'd come from Comet Creek National Park. The fire had destroyed several acres at the eastern border of Tracker Jordan's sheep station, but Officer Downs had learned that Tracker's house and outbuildings and most of his stock were all right.

After giving their statements to the officers, Frank and Joe had gone to Gil's to shower and change, while Nancy, George, Mick, and Nellie did the same at the Yungis' community. They had all met at the Flat Hill Lodge to celebrate Nellie's return and the resolution of the opal theft. Tracker, Daphne, and Harold had shown up to find out what had happened and joined the group. Regina Bourke had had to push three tables together to seat them all.

"I guess the Royces will be treating you with more respect now, Nellie," George put in. "I couldn't believe it when they actually showed up at your grandfather's house to thank you."

"I guess they realized that if it weren't for you, Gil might have gotten away with the opals," Daphne added.

"They still plan on fighting our petition to get ownership of their land," Nellie said, shaking her head. "But perhaps there is hope for a compromise."

Frank was glad that Nellie was safe, but he didn't feel nearly as happy as everyone else looked. Leaning close to Joe, he said in a low voice, "It feels weird to be celebrating the capture of one of Dad's old friends. I mean, I'm glad Nellie's safe, but . . ." His voice trailed off into a sigh. "I guess I would be *more* glad if we had caught the poacher."

"We're not done investigating yet," Joe reminded him. "First thing tomorrow, I say we search Dennis Moore's room. But for tonight, we might as well kick back. Besides, Nancy and George will be heading back to the States soon. Too bad I left my camera at Gil's. This would make a great picture."

He formed a square with his fingers, framing an imaginary shot. Then his eyes focused on something on the floor. "Hey, Harold, mind if I get a few shots with one of your cameras?"

"What?" Harold turned to Joe, then stiffened. "No. I don't think—" He reached for the aluminum carrying case, his face reddening. "That's highly specialized equipment."

Joe had already grabbed the strap from Harold's seat back and was reaching for the metal fasteners. Frank shook his head in amusement. When Joe was onto an idea, the word *no* just wasn't in his vocabulary. "Don't worry, I've used good cameras before," Joe said lightly, flipping open the lid to the case. "I know what I'm—"

He broke off and gaped into the metal case. Looking over his shoulder, Frank didn't see a single camera. The special compartment for lenses and film had been removed—revealing the pieces of a gleaming rifle in the bottom of the case. With them was a row of bullets.

"You're the poacher!" Frank blurted.

Harold jumped to his feet, sending his chair clattering to the floor. He was only a few steps away from Frank and Joe, but before they could get to him, he pulled a small gun from his jacket pocket. With lightning speed, he reached for George, who was sitting next to him.

"What?" George's cry was cut off as he locked his arm around her neck in a choke hold.

"Nobody moves!" Harold barked, holding the pistol to George's head. "If you do, your friend dies."

Chapter

Twenty-Two

G EORGE!" Seeing the terrified expression in her friend's eyes, Nancy started to jump to her feet, then froze when she saw Harold's grip tighten on the pistol.

"I said, nobody moves," he repeated. The cold, evil glint in his eyes chilled Nancy. His mild, round face had become a mask of rage.

"No one's doing anything, Harold. It's your show," Frank said. He and Joe had both frozen a few steps from Harold and were holding up their hands where he could see them. Only a few other people were in the restaurant, and they had all frozen, too. Nancy couldn't see Regina Bourke, but even if the woman called the police right away, help wouldn't arrive until it was too late.

Nancy took a few deep breaths. She had to stay

calm if she wanted to help George. "We don't want to hurt you, Harold," she said in an even voice. "Just let George go, okay?"

"Not a chance. You and your friends would be all over me in a second. Looks as if you're going to learn the hard way that I'm not the geek you thought I was," Harold said, letting out a scornful laugh. He maneuvered George to a corner near the counter, where no one could sneak up on him from behind. "Well, I've got news for you. *You're* the bumbling idiots."

Nancy exchanged a worried glance with Frank and Joe. She knew they would have to act very carefully if they wanted to save George's life. "You sure had me fooled," she told Harold, trying to sound as if she admired him. "I never suspected a thing."

"That's what Dennis Moore and I were counting on," he said proudly. "I've worked on other assignments for him with great success, and I'm not about to let a bunch of do-gooders stop me now."

At the mention of Dennis Moore's name, Nancy gazed around warily. If Moore was nearby, they could all be in even bigger trouble. Harold must have realized what she was thinking because he barked out angrily, "Moore's not here. He's at the Yungi community—not that I need him to take care of business."

"There's something I don't understand," Frank said. "If you're doing the poaching, then why is Dennis Moore here at all?"

"To throw you off my trail, naturally," Harold

scoffed. "After Gil found the rufous bettong, Dennis decided to come to Flat Hill to play the decoy. He does export aboriginal carvings as a part of his legitimate trading business, but we both knew that anyone looking into the poaching would think he was responsible regardless of what explanation he gave."

"That's why he tried to convince Regina Bourke to sell her grandfather's stuffed birds," Nancy put in. "He knew word would get back to Gil and the Hardys."

Harold nodded. "With Dennis around, who would think to suspect an unassuming photographer from Melbourne?"

"Meanwhile, you were really planning to *kill* the local wildlife, not photograph it," Joe said. "The photo assignment was totally bogus, wasn't it?"

"Keen deduction," Harold said sarcastically. His arrogance was starting to get to Nancy, but she resisted making an angry retort when she saw the fright in George's eyes.

"The rare creatures from the Comet Creek gorges would have nicely rounded out the collection of a wealthy man in Germany with whom Dennis does business," Harold explained. "The animals can be elusive, though. I needed an experienced guide to find them."

"Like Gil or Daphne," Frank supplied. "Gil must have pointed out a rufous bettong to you during your first visit into the gorges, before we arrived. That night you sneaked out of camp and killed it."

"Right you are," Harold answered.

"And when we were all camping out in the gorge, you simply pretended to go to sleep early," Daphne said.

Harold nodded. "Even the famous Hardy brothers couldn't stay on my trail. Joe didn't question it when I pretended to be disoriented. It takes only a few moments to assemble and disassemble my rifle. By the time I ran into you, it was safely stowed in my camera case. And that glorious morning when the Rover was stuck, I managed to get away and shoot that sulphur-crested cockatoo without you two suspecting a thing," he said proudly.

"Every time an animal was killed or wounded, you were there," Frank said disgustedly. Nancy could tell he was kicking himself for not making the connection sooner. "But I saw you open your case once. All I saw were compartments for lenses and film."

"A removable compartment, which snaps into the case just above my rifle," Harold informed them. "I decided to dispense with the camouflage tonight, though. With the camera equipment and the rifle, the case is heavy. But I didn't want to risk leaving the case with the rifle in my room, so I brought it with me. I can see that was a mistake."

"You pushed me off that rock ledge, didn't you?" Joe accused. "You must have checked Daphne's map and found the path linking the main trail with the waterfall trail."

"Yes. Lucky for me, that particular spot was densely overgrown." Harold readjusted his arm around George's neck, then asked, "Any more questions?"

"How were you going to transport the animals out of the outback?" Tracker asked.

A glimmer of frustration came into Harold's eyes. "I meant to wrap and bury the creatures—just long enough to make sure the buzzards wouldn't get them. I planned on coming back on my own as soon as possible to skin them and preserve the hides with an arsenic solution I've got. After that it would have been simple enough to pack up the hides and drive them back to Melbourne. The bullets I use are specially designed to do as little damage as possible to an animal's body, so the skins would have been perfect for taxidermy."

"There's one thing I don't understand," Mick spoke up. "Why make such a ruckus? Wouldn't a silencer have made sense?"

"Don't you think I thought of that?" Harold barked out. He tightened his hold around George's neck, and she gasped. "I had a silencer made for my rifle, but I lost it in the darkness the night I killed the bettong."

This guy was getting more agitated every second, Nancy realized. They had to get that gun away from him—and fast. Harold was too quick for any one of them to take on alone. But if they all worked together . . .

"I think I've done enough talking," Harold said, keeping his pistol pressed to George's temple. "I want everyone to stay still while George and I go."

Nancy shot a panicked look at Frank and Joe. She had a terrible feeling that if George left with Harold, the rest of them would never see her alive again!

A movement at the restaurant's entrance caught Nancy's eye. Turning her head, she saw Dennis Moore walk through the doorway. He did a double take when he saw Harold. "What's going on here?"

Harold whipped his head around to look at Moore. As he did so, he shifted his revolver away from George's head for the slightest instant.

That was all Joe needed. He lunged for Harold, grabbing his gun arm and wrenching it away from George.

"Hey!" Harold's cry was cut short as Daphne dove into him from his other side. She caught him around the middle, and the three of them fell in a heap to the floor next to the counter. Nancy watched just long enough to see George twist free, then she sprinted for the doorway with lightning speed.

"We can't let Moore get away!" Nancy yelled.

Dennis Moore had already bolted toward the inn's exit, but Nancy caught up to him as he reached for the door. She lashed out with a judo kick to his side, and Moore doubled over. Nancy was regaining her footing when Tracker whizzed past her and grabbed Moore's arms. Moore tried to throw off the rancher, but Mick and Nellie were right behind Tracker. Within seconds, they had Dennis Moore immobilized.

Nancy turned to the reception desk, where Regina Bourke was standing in her apron. "Lou Downs will be here any minute. You're in luck. He was at the Royces'," she told Nancy. "I sneaked out from the kitchen when I saw what was happening and called the police." Nodding at Dennis Moore, she added, "He must have slipped by while I was calling."

When Nancy stepped back into the restaurant, she saw that Frank and Joe had Harold facedown on the floor, with his arms behind his back. George and Daphne were standing next to them. "George, are you all right?" Nancy asked, running over to give her a huge hug.

"I th-think so," George answered with a shaky smile. "I'm just glad it's over. Thanks, everyone."

"It's great to know that the real poacher's been caught," Daphne said. "I hope now we can be friends again."

"Definitely," George told her.

"Nancy?" Mick called as he came back into the restaurant a few minutes later. He walked slowly over to her, George, and Daphne, a frown on his face.

"Is everything okay?" Nancy asked.

"Hmm? Oh—yes. Tracker and Regina Bourke are keeping an eye on Dennis Moore," Mick said distractedly. "There's a phone call for you. It's someone from the U.S."

"You're kidding!" Nancy shot a curious look at George, then hurried to the lobby. She passed Tracker, who was escorting Dennis Moore into the restaurant, holding Moore's arms twisted behind his back. Nancy went over to the reception desk and picked up the receiver. "Hello?"

"Hi, gorgeous."

"Ned!" Nancy could picture her boyfriend's sparkling brown eyes and handsome face. Hearing his voice, she felt a stab of homesickness. "How did you find me?"

"I got the number from your dad," Ned told her. "I'm supposed to be studying, but then I started thinking about you, and I couldn't concentrate on anything else. How's the case? Any hope of your coming home soon?"

As soon as he said the word home, Nancy longed to be back in River Heights more than anything. "Actually, we're just wrapping things up," she told him. "George and I can fly back any time."

"Good. Miss me?"

Until that moment, Nancy hadn't realized how much she *did* miss him. "Mmm. Like crazy."

They talked for only a minute longer before Nancy hung up and went back into the inn's restaurant. The Hardys had penned Harold in one of the booths, and George was talking to Daphne and Tracker at the counter. Mick was sitting by himself a few stools away from them, staring down at his hands.

"Hi," she said, sitting next to him.

He glanced up at her without saying anything. For a long moment, they just gazed at each other. "I guess you and George will be going back to the U.S. soon," Mick finally said. He didn't mention Ned, but judging by the melancholy glimmer in his eyes, Nancy guessed that he knew who had called her.

"I guess so," she answered. She wasn't sure what else to say. She had deep feelings for Mick, and coming to Australia had made her care for him more than ever. But that didn't change the fact that she had a whole life back in the States—and a boyfriend who meant even more to her than Mick.

"Mick, you're a really special person, but—"

"You don't have to say it," Mick cut in gently. He took a deep breath and let it out slowly. "Deep down, I guess I knew you'd be leaving eventually. I can't say I like it, but"—he hesitated, giving her an infectious smile—"well, fate has a way of throwing us together. You haven't seen the last of me, Nancy."

"I hope not," she said, laughing. Still, despite the special lure of Australia—and Mick Devlin—she couldn't wait to get back to Ned and the good old U.S. of A.

THE HARDY BOYS CASEFILES

Simon & Schuster Mail Order
200 Old Tappan Rd., Old Tappan, N.J. 07675

Please send me the books I have checked above. I am enclosing $_____ (please add $0.75 to cover the postage and handling for each order. Please add appropriate sales tax). Send check or money order—no cash or C.O.D.'s please. Allow up to six weeks for delivery. For purchase over $10.00 you may use VISA: card number, expiration date and customer signature must be included.

Name _____

Address _____

City _____ State/Zip _____

VISA Card # _____ Exp. Date _____

Signature _____

762-21